BUTLER'S WOMAN

EVERNIGHT PUBLISHING ®

www.evernightpublishing.com

SAM CRESCENT

Copyright© 2021

Sam Crescent

Editor: Karyn White

Cover Art: Sour Cherry Designs

Jacket Design: Jay Aheer

ISBN: 978-0-3695-0328-2

BUTLER'S WOMAN

BUTLER'S WOMAN

Chaos Bleeds, 11

Sam Crescent

Copyright © 2018

Chapter One

Butler watched Mandy's curvy as fuck ass while she wriggled it from side to side. His cock was rock-hard right now, and damn, the sight of her bent over was straight out of his dreams. He wanted her, no denying that, and he was going to have her soon. He had to have her. She'd been tormenting him for months now, and he was tired of waiting for her.

"Ouch! Fuck!"

He gritted his teeth as she came out from under the table, holding her head. She had tears in her eyes, and he quickly moved to her side.

"Are you okay?"

"No, I'm really not. Ouch, that really hurt." She rubbed her head and winced as she did. "I think it's cut. Is it cut?"

Mandy was the cleaner who had been recommended to them by Curse's old lady, Mia. From the first moment Mandy entered the club, Butler's dick suddenly had a mind of his own, and no matter what he tried to do to temper it, nothing was happening.

He was sure half of the guys in the club were laughing their asses off at his expense, but whatever. He didn't have a fucking care in the world.

Since settling down in Piston County, one after the other of his club brothers had found happiness. Devil, Ripper, Curse, Pussy, Death, Snake, Dick, Spider, Sinner, Slash, and of course Vincent.

They were all married to amazing women, and he admired them for finding the one woman for them, settling down, having a family, and just doing what they were happy with. He knew every single man in the club was happy though, and he got to witness it every single night. There was always someone around with an old lady or a couple of kids. Of course, late at night, that wasn't the case, so he was able to fuck his way through all the club whores. But in the past few months that held no appeal at all.

There was a time he'd have dealt with his problem by snorting his way through it. He'd been clean for years though, and there was no way in hell that he'd ever go down that road, so now he just drank sodas all the time and steered clear of the drugs.

Sitting Mandy down, he leaned her head forward and inspected the damage. "There's no cut."

"It hurts."

"You getting a headache?"

She closed her eyes and nodded, followed by another wince. "I think I saw a spider."

"A spider?"

"Yeah, and I jerked back, hitting my head hard."

He'd been too busy admiring the curves of her ass to really care about what was under the table.

"Shit, do you want me to check?" he asked.

"Nah, it's fine. Could you get me my washcloth though? Someone had dropped something sticky, and I was trying to clean it up."

He chuckled. "I'll also keep an eye out for the spider."

"That would be great."

Leaning under the table, he grabbed the washcloth and bucket, and saw no signs of the spider on the ground. He put the cloth into the bucket and placed them beside Mandy as she continued to rub her head.

"Thank you." She stood up, and he caught her hands.

"I think you should sit down before you injure yourself."

"I'll be fine in a couple of minutes."

"Cool, and until I'm satisfied, you're going to sit your ass down and do as I ask."

He pulled a chair in closer to her, resting his hands on her thighs. She wore a pair of old, faded jeans. The knees were looking a little worse for wear, but that was fine. He noticed Mandy didn't ever wear anything new at the club.

"What are you doing?" she asked.

"I'm keeping an eye on you. Jessica's heading over here, so she can check out your head."

She chuckled. "It's just a little bang."

"Yeah, well, I remember Sasha saying to me it was just a fall and she was blind for several years until she had another bang."

"I've met Sasha. She's a nice woman." Mandy groaned. "I didn't know she was blind though."

"She's not now, but when I first met her, she was."

"Wow, that's kind of surreal."

"Yeah, bangs on the head are no joking matter. You need to learn to take care of yourself."

She chuckled. "Yes, sir."

"I like that. I like being a sir."

"I really need this job."

"You're not going to lose it."

"What about Devil?"

"He won't fire you because you hit your head."

"Thank you," she said.

"For what?"

"For being nice to me. It's … I like it." She smiled at him, and he saw the pain in her eyes which he didn't think was from the bang to the head.

"I'm really sorry about your mom."

She bit her lip, and he saw tears in her eyes. Mandy had left the Chaos Bleeds clubhouse for several months, and none of them had known why until she came to Devil, asking for her job back. Her stepfather had murdered her mother, and they'd placed Mandy in protective custody, which he had been and was now behind bars. Reaching out, Butler tucked a curl of brown hair behind her ear.

"Thank you."

"It must be hard without her at times."

"I don't know. We never got along. I didn't like her choice in men, so after a big argument I stormed out and never returned until I got the call that her body was in the morgue."

"It's not your fault." He saw that she blamed herself.

"Maybe not but we never got to make amends." She pressed her lips together, and it made him just want to hug her, to hold her tight.

"I didn't know your mom, but I don't think anyone would want their child to live with guilt for what wasn't said in life."

She chuckled. "She could be quite spiteful when she wanted to be."

"Then the bitch ain't worth your time."

"Thank you," she said. "For cheering me up."

He laughed. "Really? I feel I'm making you even more sad." *What the fuck are you? A pussy?*

"Nah, it's fine. Honestly. I appreciate what you're saying." She held her head and groaned.

"Are you okay?"

"Yeah, of course, I'm fine."

"Let me go and see if Jessica has gotten in yet." He patted her knee, needing to do something otherwise he was going to lose his mind.

He found Jessica in the main club room. She still had her little girl in her arms, and a bag on her shoulder. She'd given birth two months ago to Bell.

"Hey, can you come and check on Mandy?" he asked.

"What's up?" Jessica asked, dropping the bag to the floor.

"She banged her head underneath the table, and she doesn't look so good."

"You know I'm on maternity leave, right?"

"Yeah, but you're a nurse all the time. You'll never allow someone to be hurt."

"That's very true," she said, cooing at her little girl. "Have you seen Snake?"

"No. Here, I'll hold her while you go and check out Mandy." He held his arms out, and Jessica raised a brow.

"Really?"

"Yes, I don't mind."

"Thanks." She eased Bell into his arms, and the little girl snuggled in close and he smiled down at her.

Babies were the cutest thing in the world, and he just adored them. He didn't see himself having any, but then he also didn't see himself getting to forty with the way his life was going.

He'd been one of the first brothers in the club to enter himself into a rehab clinic, but that hadn't been a fucking easy decision to make. In fact, it had been really hard. For so long his life had been about the drugs, the booze, the whores, and just having a good time. He didn't give a shit if he didn't remember anything of the day before, or the night, or even if he didn't know who he'd fucked.

The fact he'd been able to stay clean, no STIs or STDs in sight, was a fucking miracle. The lifeline Devil gave to him, he'd taken it. One day he'd woken up in a bed of six women, and he didn't remember anything. He'd been surrounded by empty bottles and a dusting of coke on the table where lines had been done.

He couldn't remember exactly what happened, just that he knew he had to stop. He didn't want a life spent in a blurry haze. So, he'd gotten his shit together, and now he was so fucking happy. Happier than he'd been in a long time.

Following Jessica back to Mandy, he watched as she went to work, asking questions and checking the site. The club always had available the first aid kit that Jessica requested, and she already wore a pair of latex gloves.

After a few seconds Jessica smiled. "You'll be fine. You hit your head pretty hard though. Be careful, okay."

"I will. Thank you."

"No problem." She removed her gloves and placed them in the waste basket. "Can I have my little girl now, even though she looks so sweet and snuggly in Uncle Butler's arms?"

He chuckled. "Here you go, mama."

"That never gets old." Jessica smiled at him and left them alone.

****

Mandy watched as Butler took a seat before her. He reached out, touching her head. "You okay?"

"Yes, I'm fine. Thank you."

She liked Butler. He was a nice man. She knew from listening to several women that he was an ex-addict. Her curiosity about him had gotten the better of her and she'd asked Mia a few questions, but the other woman wasn't a gossip.

Mandy figured it had to be something about the club as a whole.

He kept staring at her as if he wanted to ask her something. Finally feeling a little uncomfortable, she got to her feet. He did the same, his hands opening and closing. His body seemed to vibrate.

"Thank you so much for taking care of me."

"You're welcome."

Picking up her bucket, she gave him one last lingering smile before leaving the room. She didn't understand why he made her nervous. Out of all of the men she'd known, Butler did something to her. Words always failed her, and she had never been accused of being quiet.

"Hey, Jessica just told me what happened. Are you okay?" Mia asked, coming to her.

"Yeah, I'm fine. Occupational hazard and all that. You know, banging head on the table."

"Yeah, I remember. Are you out for the night?"

Mia was a sweet woman. Mandy knew that she'd had it rough with her friend dying, and problems with the club. They were friends but not close. Their only real connection was their cleaning work and that was how she got this job.

"Yeah, I'm about to head home."

Butler came out of the room, and for some strange reason her cheeks heated at the sight of him. Forcing herself to look away, she took a deep breath and concentrated on what Mia was saying.

"What do you think?" Mia asked.

"I'm so sorry, what?"

Mia chuckled. "Butler does have that effect on a lot of women."

"I'm fine." She'd been saying that a lot lately, and even she was tired of hearing about it. "I'm sorry. It has been a long day. I don't even know what came over me."

"Have you found a place in Piston County?"

"Not yet. I'm still looking for a place that I can afford." After her stepfather was jailed for killing her mother, Mandy had decided to move to Piston County for good. There was no point being away, and she made some decent money with her cleaning work. She liked cleaning, and of course it helped to pay the bills. The best gig was the Chaos Bleeds clubhouse. Without a doubt they were some of the scruffiest men she'd ever had to clean up after.

She didn't mind at all. Most of the men left her alone. She noticed that Butler was always hanging around, staring at her. There were times it was like he wanted to ask her something, but she didn't know what.

"If you want I can ask Devil? He tends to know everything and everyone," Mia said.

"That's sweet, but I can really find my own way." She touched Mia's arm. "I'm going to head out. Have a good weekend."

It was Friday night, and she just wanted to get home, put her feet up, and forget about all of her troubles, past, present, future.

She filled the trunk of her car with her supplies and was about to climb inside just as Devil came out.

"I heard you hit your head," he said.

"Oh, it's fine. Did Butler tell you?"

"No, Jessica did. You're sure you're okay? I could have one of the guys take you home."

"It was just a bump."

"Still, I'm not willing to risk it. Stay there."

She should just get in her car, but instead she watched the Prez of Chaos Bleeds make his way inside. She didn't know what he intended to do, but arguing with Devil didn't seem like the right thing to do. That man commanded respect from everywhere. There were times she looked at him and was sure he held the door that was the gateway to hell. Her thoughts were driving her crazy even now.

Seconds later he came out, followed by Butler.

"He's going to take you home," Devil said.

"That's really not necessary."

"I don't care what you think is necessary or not. It's what is happening." Devil slapped Butler on the back. "He doesn't mind taking you home."

She watched Devil climb into his car and take off.

"You really don't have to. I feel fine."

"It's no big deal. I was only sitting around reading."

"Oh, what were you reading?" She loved a good book herself. Seeing as all her cash was going into a savings account for a place to stay, she borrowed all of her books from the library.

"It's a crime thriller thing. I don't know. I've only just started it, but it's boring as shit."

"Okay. I can see why you think that." She nodded her head pressing her lips together.

"What kind of books are you into then?"

"I like romance ones. I know it's totally lame." She actually loved dirty, sexy books, but right now, she'd take what she could get. A little romance never hurt anyone, and Butler didn't need to know what she craved.

"It's not lame. You like what you like." He moved toward her side and gripped the door. "You're not driving this car, Mandy. You may as well stop fighting me."

"This is my baby."

"And I will take care of it. Believe me. You'll get home in one piece. That I can promise you."

She sighed and moved around to the passenger side, climbing in.

It had been a long time since anyone drove her home or at all. She'd gotten used to taking care of herself.

"Are you okay over there?" he asked, getting behind the wheel.

"Yeah, I'm fine, of course." She forced a smile and blew out a breath. "Everything is more than good."

"You totally hate me in your car right now, don't you?"

"It's fine."

"You can hate me. I don't mind."

She laughed. "I'm so used to driving myself it just seems wrong that you're here. I can't even believe we're talking about something like this. It's a little stupid."

He chuckled, and she liked the sound. "You'll do fine. So, what is it you like about romance?"

"I don't know. The men are always dreamy and know what to do." Her cheeks heated, and she quickly added. "You know, with roses and stuff." He didn't need to know that the men in the books knew exactly how to please a woman. She really did wish all men were like that. That all it took was one look at the right man, and he could make you sing all the way through your orgasm.

She gave him directions to where she was staying.

"Some men are like that."

"Like what?" she asked.

"The roses and stuff. Devil is constantly showing Lexie how much he loves and appreciates her."

Lexie was Devil's old lady, and from what she heard, he had kept her barefoot and pregnant for a long time.

She'd also seen them together, and there was no doubt in her mind that he loved her. It was the kind of love people wrote about and everyone wished they had. She wasn't jealous of them at all.

Relationships were not something Mandy was good at, and she didn't see herself having one for a long time. In fact, she'd sworn off men and sex for so long as she didn't trust herself with either. Sex was something she'd been addicted to and had always kept it casual, like one night with a stranger. She wasn't going to go back to that way of sleeping with strangers.

Being in the clubhouse she'd been exposed to some of the guys that weren't married and their sexual exploits. She'd not been shocked by what she'd seen, but she had wished to be part of it, only she didn't want to be another pussy in a group of them. She'd seen the difference between the old ladies and the club whores, and she didn't want to be a random pussy to be used by anyone who wanted a turn.

Something casual wasn't like before, was it? Sex with strangers was different from having someone to sleep with. She was so confused.

"You're here," Butler said.

"Oh, I'm so sorry. I completely zoned out there."

"It's fine."

He parked the car and climbed out. She noticed he was moving to her door, and she gasped as he opened it, holding out a hand. "Come on."

"You're being the perfect gentleman."

"I know how to act." He gave her a wink and took her to the front door. Opening the lock, she glanced back at him, suddenly feeling this overwhelming urge to kiss him.

"Thank you for bringing me home. How are you getting back?"

"One of the boys is taking me. Don't worry." He stepped back, and any opportunity to kiss him was missed.

Forcing a smile, she gave him a wave, closing the door.

"What the hell just happened?"

Chapter Two

One week later

Butler watched as Tiny and Devil shook hands. Out of the corner of his eye he saw Tabitha and Simon on the set of swings at the clubhouse. They were growing up so fast. Every single summer they made several trips to Fort Wills, or The Skulls came to Piston County for a visit. They had picnics, rides out, and just shot the shit together.

This was one of those times when they were talking business, only their life was no longer drugs or guns, or their enemies that came at them from all angles.

For a long time, they'd all had to sleep with one eye open, and that shit was fucking dangerous.

It was one of the reasons he decided to get clean before Devil ordered the ban. Some of the men had followed orders, Dick being one of them. Of course, there were also men who'd left the club. Handed in their patch, blacked out their colors, and gone on their merry way.

Butler couldn't do it.

He couldn't hand his life's loyalty over like that. The drugs had been part of him for so long that quitting had seemed like an asshole thing to do. They were what made his life bearable.

"Are you okay?" Natalie asked, taking a seat beside him. He sat at one of the garden tables that Lexie had been sure to purchase for them all. Steaks were on the grill, the kids dancing around merrily, and he, like always, was lost in thought.

Natalie was one of the few people he actually called a friend.

He'd tried to win her from Slash, but that had been a fucking mistake as far as Butler was concerned.

"Yeah, I'm fine. What are you doing over here?" he asked. "And where is your precious little son?"

Natalie had given birth to a little boy, Thomas, not so long ago. Slash had never looked so damn happy as when he was carrying his son.

"Slash has got him."

"Yeah, totally proud he is, isn't he?" Butler asked.

"He is. I hear him at night when he's reading to him. There's always wonder in his voice. 'I made you. Me and mommy made you.'" She giggled. "It's so cute. I mean seriously so."

He laughed. "I bet you're loving it."

"We are."

He glanced down at his glass.

"What's wrong, Butler?"

"Nothing. I'm all good here. You know."

"No, you're not. Something is bothering you. Is this to do with Mandy?" she asked.

"Yeah, it is. I want her, you know." He wanted Mandy, but it was the last thing on his mind right now. He couldn't stop looking at the soda in front of him or catching the old marks from his years of using.

Life had slowed down. It had gotten easier, and with it ... he felt something he hadn't felt in years, and that was scaring the fuck out of him.

"You know you could ask her out. She's not seeing anyone. At least she's not the last time I asked."

"Are you wanting to date our cleaner as well?"

"Totally. I see a threesome on the cards with Slash every single day." Natalie gave that little chuckle that made him smile.

Natalie was a sweet, loving girl.

He enjoyed her company, and he couldn't believe he'd nearly ruined their friendship by thinking for a second that he wanted her that way. He didn't.

She was just nice, and he liked nice.

Nice is boring and easy.

"I better go. You see the way Devil and Tiny are constantly watching their kids." Natalie placed a hand on his arm before leaving.

Glancing over at the swings, he watched as Simon moved behind Tabitha, pulled back the swing, and started pushing her. Tabitha wore a pair of jeans and a shirt. There wasn't a big age gap between them. Simon and Tabitha had always been close, even though it sometimes annoyed Tiny and Devil about what it could mean for the future of their kids. At one point it was a concern for the future of both clubs as Tiny had been the Prez, but right now, it was Lash that was Prez, so all eyes turned to Anthony, Lash's son.

Their visits between the clubs had brought the two kids together. Tiny had once been the Prez of The Skulls until he handed the gavel over to Lash. Pressures within the club had brought about a tension between theirs and a change in leadership had helped to draw them close together again.

I could really use a fucking hit.

Butler's hands clenched into tight fists. It had been a long time since he'd gotten that craving, that sudden calling.

Watching the innocence of love, and knowing the club had changed paths for good, something was changing within him. Chaos Bleeds helped to provide backup for The Skulls when they were helping women in abusive, dangerous situations. They became a safehouse for them, and Devil had also become part of it, much to the anger of Ned Walker.

That old fart was going to outlive them all, and laugh to his fucking grave as he did.

Running fingers through his hair, Butler quickly finished his soda and made his way toward the front of the clubhouse.

No one was around, and, straddling his bike, he pulled out of the clubhouse. He didn't bother with a helmet; he never did.

Riding through the roads, he overtook cars and traveled up toward the large mountain that overlooked the town.

A lot of high school kids had started using the point to make out and for fucking at night. He simply avoided it then.

It wasn't on his list of shit to do to watch a couple of horny kids fuck.

Parking his bike, he climbed off and moved toward the well-worn picnic table that was there. Folding his legs, he sat as if he was at school on the mat waiting for a story.

I want a fucking hit.

I want oblivion.

They don't need me.

Running his hand across his face, he couldn't believe the constant need that was building within him.

When life was going to shit, he didn't have the time to think about what was happening or what he was missing out on.

Now life was normal.

It was easy.

They didn't need him to focus anymore.

He placed his hands on his knees and tried to meditate, to think of something else, and Mandy's face popped into his mind, which didn't help matters for him. She didn't help to clear his mind.

Any other time in his life he'd have chased after her, no problem. As it was, he couldn't do it.

He was too fucked up in the head to give her that chance.

Slapping his head, he took a deep breath and forced himself to focus.

This was his life, and he wasn't about to screw that up.

Sweat covered his skin, and he stared out across Piston County. This was his home. Where his Prez had found his son and the woman of his dreams. Over the years he'd watched his friends and club brothers fall. One by one they'd given in to temptation, and now here he sat.

All alone.

The club was in the best position it ever had been.

No more dangerous runs that could get them killed or locked up.

They had numerous businesses around the town from real estate, fashion shops, warehouses, titty clubs, the works. On the side they helped The Skulls protect people.

Life was fucking normal.

And yet, as life was starting to look so good, he was staring to fall apart, and it was driving him crazy this constant fire that burned within him.

Mandy had been through hell and back. He knew because he got Whizz on one of his trips to do a thorough background check. The mother had put Mandy in and out of care growing up to suit her. Not only that, there were several police reports where Mandy had accused her mother's boyfriends of touching and being inappropriate. What pissed him off was the fact the mother claimed her daughter was a slut, and was asking for it.

He knew every single little detail of Mandy's life, from her savings, to the fact she wanted to get a place. He didn't need to hear Mia tell him her life story, or what she was doing. He was that fucking obsessed with her, he already knew.

This was just another reason why he couldn't go chasing after Natalie. She hadn't been the girl that made him go to Whizz to find everything out. She didn't keep him awake at night thinking about if she was okay. She certainly didn't make him think twice about his current fucking problem.

He needed a hit, and there was no chance in hell of letting Mandy know what kind of shit he was in.

****

"Well, you're a sexy lady," a guy with a British accent said.

Mandy finished scrubbing the last of the toilet and turned to look to see a guy she didn't recognize. He wasn't wearing the Chaos Bleeds patch, and she just smiled.

Mia had told her that several of The Skulls men were staying in Piston County for a week or so.

"Thank you."

"And you've got one of the prettiest voices."

She chuckled.

"Stop trying to woo the woman," Ripper said, coming into the room. "Devil wants to see you, Mandy."

"The pretty lady has a name."

Her cheeks heated as Ripper rolled his eyes. "The British guy is Adam. Adam, this is Mandy. She's not for you to play around with."

Pulling off her glove, she shook Adam's hand. "It's nice to meet you."

"If you want to break the rules, I'd be more than happy to play with you."

Again, she laughed. He seemed like the kind of guy who liked to have a lot of fun.

"That's not going to happen. I like my job."

"Shame. If you change your mind in the next week, I'll be here and waiting."

Ripper sighed, and she pulled her cleaning supplies from the toilet.

"Time for me to use the bog."

She frowned, leaving the room. "Bog?"

"He's British."

"Okay." She knew they had weird words for things but seriously? She'd never heard a toilet be referred to as a bog. "Have I done something wrong?" she asked, following behind him.

"Not that I know of."

Ripper led her to Devil's office, and she bit her lip, suddenly really nervous about being here right now.

It's fine. You're fine.

Knocking on the door, she waited for Devil to respond. The moment he did, Ripper gave her a smile before leaving.

The club was a lovely place to be, which considering they're an MC club, was saying a lot. Yes, they were messy and they fucked a lot, drank a lot, but she loved them.

Entering the office, she saw Devil sitting behind his desk. He wore a pair of glasses that were perched on his nose.

"Hey, Mandy, come on in."

She closed the door and made her way toward the chair opposite his desk. Sitting down, she felt like she was seeing the principal or something.

Biting her lip, she waited for him to speak up.

"I've been made aware that you're looking for a place to stay."

"Oh, well, I am, but it's not a problem." In fact, it had gone up in her list of priorities as her friend who was allowing her to rent the place she was currently in had told her she was in the process of selling it and needed her to leave as soon as possible. That's what good friends were all about. Dumping you at the deep end and leaving you to fend for yourself.

It wasn't a problem.

She had hoped to get the rest of the year as had been originally planned. Her friend had said that she wasn't doing anything with the place until then.

Now that had all changed.

"I am looking for somewhere."

"Excellent. We have a place. It's fully paid for. You can rent it from us, and I will do you a good deal." He opened the drawer and pulled out a file. "If you'd like to take a look."

She took the file and looked through. It was a luxury place.

"The club purchased the building a couple of years ago. With Spider's help we've been working on getting the apartments finished. Mia told Lexie about your current situation, and I listen to my wife. We like you at the club. I trust you, and I know you've had a hard time of it. I want to help you out." He gave her a figure of the rent, and she gasped.

"Are you serious right now?"

"Totally serious."

"Oh, my, I can't even begin to believe this." There were two bedrooms, a nice-sized kitchen, bathroom, dining room, sitting room, and it was fully furnished. "This is amazing. I can't believe…"

"Do you want it?" Devil asked. "I won't be offended if you don't want it."

"Yes, I want it. I've not been able to find anything that would be worth this, and this is so amazing." Her heart was racing. She couldn't believe this was happening. "Thank you. Yes, where do I sign?"

He chuckled. "Lexie's waiting out in the car. If you want we'll drive you over there right now and get you started on everything."

Within minutes she was in the car, and they were driving toward the apartment building. It was about thirty minutes from the club, and not far from the town either, which was good. She liked being able to travel but not overly long distances.

Lexie and Devil talked about the kids with random little comments about the apartment.

When they came to a stop outside of the building, she smiled. Already she loved it.

"We've been investing in the locals, giving them the opportunity to work," Devil said.

"This is amazing."

Leaving the car, she followed Lexie and Devil up to the apartment. They stood in the elevator, and she watched the two hold hands. Devil's much bigger hand locked fingers with Lexie's.

The power and love between these two were just amazing to witness. She'd seen them together for some time now, and they were the two that held the club together. Lexie dealt with all the women, from the old ladies to the club whores, while Devil didn't miss a thing and made sure to keep his men in line. The couple was loved and respected.

The elevator doors opened, and Mandy walked out.

Devil held the key, and he slid it into the lock, opening up the door.

The windows were floor to ceiling, and the views were just beautiful. Stepping into the room, she felt like she'd walked into an alternate universe. There was no way something like this could ever happen to her.

"Everything is fully furnished," Lexie said.

"My woman has that job. She picks everything out."

"The old ladies pretty much furnish the entire thing. Top to bottom. It's top of the range, and seeing as Devil owns the place—"

"We own it. The club does."

"Then you'll always be able to find the person to complain to," Lexie said.

"Are you two serious right now? I don't think I've ever lived anywhere so grand and fine. I mean, I feel like a princess right now." She was used to damp, mold, and insects. Maybe even a few rats from some of her living accommodations. "Can I take it, like, right now? I would totally love to move in."

She moved to stand in front of them.

Lexie was laughing.

"I'll call the boys to bring your stuff up," Devil said.

"Wait, you already have my stuff?"

"I kind of took your keys. We knew that you were having a hard time," Lexie said. "I hope you're not mad."

"Any other time I would so be mad, but there's no way I can be. I mean, look at this place."

Devil was already making the call, and within seconds the men were bringing up her boxed belongings.

It had been a long time since she'd been excited about something like this. She didn't want to look like a total loser in front of them, so she tried with all her might to contain it. Once her stuff was in her place, she called her friend to let her know she was out, and didn't have to worry. She already had the key in the mail, and that was another part of her life closed.

Mandy was always closing doors on parts of her life. It made a change to finally be opening them.

After all of her boxes were in the apartment, the

men left. Lexie pulled her into a hug. "If you need anything, don't fail to ask for help. We'll be here for you."

"I know." She'd never ask for help. That wasn't her style. She was the kind of girl that always did her own thing and took care of herself. That wasn't going to change. "Thank you so much for this."

"Enjoy it."

Closing the door, she clicked the locks into place. Not that she had any doubt about the Chaos Bleeds' security, but locking her door was a habit. She had gotten into the habit after one of her stints in foster care when one of the boys there hadn't taken no for an answer. He'd only barged into her room once and nearly took what she wasn't offering.

Leaning against the door, she smiled.

Something like this never happened to her, but she wasn't about to doubt the reason for it, or why.

"Taking a deep breath, she stared at her meager belongings and didn't care. This was her place, and she was about to make it home.

****

Later that night Lexie rubbed some cream into her hands as she entered her bedroom. Devil was on the bed, looking through a tablet. Ever since Whizz had showed him how easy it was to keep an eye on not only the club but all of his businesses, he took that damn device everywhere.

"How is everything?" Lexie asked.

"It's looking okay. The club's fine. Naked Fantasies has too many customers, so I'm going to deal with that." He tutted and clicked the tablet closed before smiling up at her. "Simon is still in his bedroom?"

"Of course," she said.

Devil stared at her.

"They're having a sleepover," Lexie said. "They're camping out, and you don't have to worry."

"I worry about the fact Tabitha is currently sleeping with my son in his bed."

Lexie rolled her eyes. "Right now, it's all innocent."

"He loves her, and I'm too young to be a grandpa."

She burst out laughing. "You're going to have to deal with being one soon. At this rate, Ned will be the sexiest grandpa around. In fact, he'd be the sexiest great-grandpa."

"Yeah, well right now he's having a temper tantrum."

"He's still not come around with the changes?" Lexie asked, climbing into bed.

Devil wasn't having any of that. He lifted her up so that she was straddling him, where she found her sexy husband had no pants on. His naked cock pressed against her pussy, and she closed her eyes.

"You know, no matter how many times I fuck you, or see you naked, or watch how dirty you can get, I still want you."

Wrapping her arms around his neck, she pressed her lips against his cheek. "You love it."

He ran his hands down her back, grabbing the negligee and lifting it up over her head so that she was completely naked. He ran his hands all over her body, cupping her tits before sliding down to cup her ass.

"These are fucking heaven and all mine." He gripped her ass tightly, and she whimpered, not wanting him to stop.

"Do you think Mandy is going to be good for Butler?" she asked.

Her meddling husband had his ways of knowing

what his club needed and wanted. He'd noticed a change in Butler in the past few weeks, and since then, he'd been working on keeping Mandy close.

She was the only woman that Butler had shown any real interest in.

"Yes. Something has got to give, and I think the two of them together will make a fantastic couple. Now, enough talk about men and women. It's time for me to fuck my wife so she knows exactly who she belongs to."

Chapter Three

"Then you cross that braid with that one, and then again, and again," Tabitha said. "See, it's not so bad."

Butler forced a smile as he was on babysitting duty at Lexie and Devil's home. Tabitha, all of Devil's kids, all of Eva's, and it was just a mass of kids everywhere. He'd put the youngest in a small play area, and the older kids were either in the kitchen or at the dining room table. Tabitha had decided that he needed to be taught how to do a braid, not that he'd ever need to do it.

"You look cute," Simon said.

"You need to learn to do it as well, Simon." Tabitha removed her braid and turned her back to Simon.

"What is your fascination with hair?" Daisy asked.

Daisy was Whizz and Lacey's daughter. He also had their newly adopted son, who was asleep in one of the cribs. Whizz and Lacey had taken a much-needed vacation, and, seeing as Eva and Tiny offered to take the kids and they were in Piston County, Butler was taking care of them.

"I don't know. I love it." Tabitha gasped. "Maybe I should be, like, a hairstylist or something."

Simon picked up the brush and began to run it through her hair.

Deciding he needed another cup of coffee, Butler made his way into the kitchen where he saw Anthony eating some chips. Anthony was Lash and Angel's son. There were so many fucking kids he couldn't believe he kept notice at all.

"You okay, son?" Butler asked.

"Yeah, fine."

"What's wrong?"

"I don't know. Darcy's tired again. She's sleeping upstairs." Anthony frowned.

"Did you guys stay up late last night?"

"No. She's always tired lately, and she's pale."

"I'm sure it's nothing."

Darcy was one of the oldest of The Skulls kids.

Next time babysitting duty came around he was going to fucking demand another job. Kids were not his thing.

There was a knock at the door, and he was just happy to get away from all the kids. At least several of the older ones helped out with the younger ones, which worked for him.

Opening the door, he was surprised to see Mandy there.

"Mandy," he said.

"Devil said you needed help." She held up a large bag of takeout food. "I think he said the house was being taken over by a bunch of kids and that if I didn't help you, you'd come back and haunt me."

Butler chuckled. "It's not too bad, but I somehow got this gig and everyone just got to go out. I need to learn to keep my mouth shut."

Opening the door wider, he allowed her to enter. The scent of Chinese food brought the kids toward them. Most of them were The Skulls, but coming up behind them were Paul, Simon, and Elizabeth.

"Kids, this is Mandy. Mandy, this is all the kids. Unless I put a sticker on them, it's complicated to say who is who."

Simon chuckled. "It's pretty simple. Miles, Tabby, and Luke are Tiny's. Anthony and Chloe belong to Lash."

"Yeah, yeah, I'm done, and I'm bored," Butler said. "Let's eat."

With Mandy's help, he got all the kids fed, and she even came with soda. It wasn't long before they were all happily in the large sitting room and they were watching a movie. Having all the kids crowded in one room, he placed his hands on his hips, proud of what he'd achieved.

Mandy stood beside him with a huge smile on her face. "I didn't know you guys had so many kids."

"They're both The Skulls and Chaos Bleeds. They're all good friends though." He noticed Simon and Tabitha curled up together holding hands. *Young love.*

He rubbed at his eyes, suddenly feeling tired. "Come on, I'll make us some coffee."

He made his way back into the kitchen and started up some coffee.

"They're all really good," Mandy said.

"Yeah, they know not to mess up Devil's house. A few years ago, they were all here, and it was a complete disaster. They completely trashed the place, and he made them all do chores with a whistle and all. Everyone who grumbled got the shitty jobs." He chuckled, recalling how much the kids hated it.

"Devil seems to know what to do to keep everyone in line."

"That's the truth. He's a good man like that. How's your new place?"

"It's awesome. I can't believe how I've been able to live everywhere else."

"You lived in some bad places?" he asked, making it a question rather than showing that he knew the truth. She didn't need to know that he was completely obsessed by her, and that he knew every little detail of her life.

"Yeah, really bad. In some places there were more rats than humans." She smiled. "I can't even believe I'm smiling about this. It seems kind of surreal to go from there to now. I tell you, I'd let my younger self know that shit gets better." She covered her mouth. "Sorry, I didn't mean to cuss."

"They can cuss better than you, believe me." He placed a cup of coffee in front of her.

"You seem to totally handle them all. There was no screaming or anything. Do you want kids?" she asked.

"No."

"Wow, that was … quick. Just a plain and simple no."

"Kids are not for me." He glanced down at his scars from the years of abuse he'd given himself. "You?"

"Erm, no, not really. It's not something I've ever thought about, in all honesty."

"How come?"

She wrinkled her nose. "Bad childhood, I guess. My mom wasn't the best when it came to raising her kid. I loved her, and she tried in her own way. It wasn't enough, and here I am now."

"I think you turned out okay."

"Yeah, it wasn't always bad, you know. There were some rough patches. A lot of people go through them."

"That I know for certain."

At this her gaze went to his arms. "You're an ex-addict."

"According to the program I'm always an addict. Temptation is always there. Just got to fight to get rid of it."

"Is that one of the reasons you don't want kids?"

"There's always a risk of falling off the wagon, always. I don't want to risk that kind of life for any kid of mine. It's not worth it."

"Did you get free yourself?"

"Yeah, I did. At the time it felt like the best thing to do."

"You don't think it's a good thing?"

"A lot of shit was going down at the club. Can't talk about it, but I needed to be clean. Devil, the club, they all needed me. I did my time."

"And now?"

"Now, nothing."

"It doesn't sound like nothing, Butler. It sounds like you're waiting." She reached out, touching his arm. "Talk to me."

"There's nothing to talk about." He finished his scalding hot liquid. "Just got to keep moving forward. To keep every single day ticking on by."

"I'm always here if you want to talk to me. I know what it's like to feel like you're going crazy."

"You fell off a wagon? Took some shit?"

"No, I've never done any of that."

"Then what?"

"I used to go around looking for fights," she said. Okay, this shocked him.

"What?"

"In high school, when I was in and out of foster care. I don't know, I went a bit crazy. I started carrying around a knife, and I'd walk the streets. When I think back to some of the things I did, it scares me. I would go up to the biggest person I could find, and I'd try and get them to hurt me. To kick, to make me feel something other than rage. I was filled with it. Got into a lot of scrapes. I never ended up in the hospital though. Just went home with black eyes, bruised ribs, that kind of thing."

"Wow," Butler said.

"Yeah. I think it really came from anger. I couldn't hurt my mom, and she always found a way to hurt me. If I hit her, she put me in foster care. I didn't like that. It was the last thing I wanted."

Butler wanted to hug her, to hold her and let her know that everything would be okay, but that wasn't his place. She wasn't his woman.

"Have you thought of talking to someone?"

"Don't worry about it," he said. "I'm fine. This is just one of those things that will pass." He tapped the counter and forced a smile. "I better go and check on them."

Leaving the kitchen, he stood outside of the sitting room and rested his head against the wall. Right now, he was hanging on by a thread. He needed something to ground him, to help take the edge off, but nothing was happening.

He didn't want to talk to Devil or worry the club, nor did he want to go back to rehab.

Something had to give, but he was afraid of what happened when it did.

****

The next couple of days Mandy didn't know what to do about her talk with Butler. He was a good man, but she saw that he was struggling with something. His past addiction clearly seemed to be the problem.

She was cleaning up the clothing store that the Chaos Bleeds owned in town. Several women were trying on clothes, and Lexie stood behind the counter going through accounts. Finishing up the back, Mandy made her way out of the shop, putting away her cleaning equipment. She always kept it with her in case of a phone call and a last-minute job. As Mandy entered the shop, Lexie was already waiting for her.

"I figured we could do lunch today if you're not too busy."

"I'd love to. I've got to head over to the

clubhouse this afternoon."

Lexie shook her head. "I don't know how you can still smile after working in that place. I know from personal experience that some of the guys are just downright nasty."

She chuckled. "It's not too bad most of the time." She wasn't about to bring up the used condoms. They were the reason she wore latex gloves.

Sitting behind the counter, Mandy watched as the women kept coming in and out of the changing room.

"Natalie's a real star, isn't she?" Lexie said.

"Yeah. She has a keen eye."

"If you'd like, you could have a couple of shifts at the shop. We wouldn't mind sharing the workload with you."

"I thought this was for the old ladies?"

"It is, but you're a friend."

"Thank you."

"Don't mention it. I'd appreciate the help from time to time. I come here to get away from the kids and to have a few hours away."

"You have got a lot of kids," she said, recalling the full sitting room.

"How did you enjoy spending time with Butler and the herd? You never did say?"

"It was fine. They were all well behaved."

"Butler included?"

"Yes, he was the best." She took a bite of her sandwich, trying not to think about all of the other bad things that Butler could do. "How is he?"

"Butler?"

"Yes."

"He's fine. Why do you ask?"

"I was just worried. He seems more withdrawn than normal. I didn't know if that was normal Butler or not."

"He's never been the most talkative. Life has taken a lot of dramatic turns for the club."

"I had heard rumors that you guys haven't had an easy time of it." She watched as Lexie sighed.

"Yeah. Marrying Devil was like the dream I never thought I had, if that makes any sense at all. He was a biker, and I was just the girl with a ba—trying to deal with everything. Then he came into my world, and everything changed. With the problems the clubs were having, I don't think I even got to stop and enjoy being married. It was just one thing after another, after another."

"You both love each other though. You can clearly see that."

"Oh, I do. I love him more than anything. Our little family is perfect for me. No more kids though. We're all kidded out."

"You've got a nice little brood," Mandy said.

"If you do have any concerns about Butler, talk to Devil. He will listen. He's not always mean. That just seems to come naturally to him."

"He does seem quite scary, doesn't he?" Mandy said.

"Not to me."

They finished their lunch, and Mandy got up and didn't know what to do as Lexie hugged her. She'd never been a touchy-feely kind of person with anyone. Patting Lexie's back, she forced a smile before saying goodbye.

She'd never been able to connect with many people in her life, what with being in and out of the foster care system, a mother who jumped from bed to bed, and a life that just always seemed to take her in the wrong direction.

Firing up her car, Mandy made her way toward

the clubhouse, wondering what she should do. Her conversations with Butler were rarely anything to write home about. They talked about everything and nothing, so she didn't understand her worries right now.

Entering the clubhouse with her supplies, she paused at the mess.

She didn't work weekends as that was when a lot of parties usually happened. Staring at the mess right now, she couldn't believe this place was completely spick and span when she left it.

"You had a good party?" she asked, passing Dime. He was splayed on the counter.

"It was one hell of a party. You should have been here, cleaner. You'd have loved it."

Moving on, she didn't linger, and instead made her way upstairs. She may as well start as she meant to go on. Devil and Lexie's room was always the cleanest, and so after a quick buzz of the carpets, and some dusting, she was done. Moving down a level, several doors were locked, so she left them.

Devil told her to clean every single room that the door was open to. Any that were locked, she left.

It made for some really startling discoveries. Sex, plain and simple; naked men who had passed out. The sights went on and on.

Getting to one of the bedrooms on the third floor, she opened the door and stopped.

Butler sat on the floor, his legs spread out. A table was in front of him, and on that table was a bag of white powder.

Mandy had never seen drugs in the clubhouse, and knowing that he was once an addict, she felt sick to her stomach.

"Don't go," Butler said when she turned to leave.

Her heart was racing as she looked at him.

"Close the door."

This was a turning point.

She *should* go and get Devil so that he could fix this and she wouldn't have to worry.

Instead, she put her cleaning items down and closed the door. This time she locked it.

"That's drugs," she said.

"No shit."

"You bought them?"

"That's usually the way, isn't it? I went and bought them this morning. Looking at them right now." He held up one hand. "This guy is telling me to take them. That it'll be easy and it would solve all of my fucking problems." He lowered one hand only to raise the other. "And this one is telling me that I'm a fucking useless prick, and that if I take this would be causing all manner of problems."

"Why did you buy them?" she asked, stepping into the room. She moved so that she stood in front of them.

"Because everything is going great and I … can't seem to stop thinking about them. My head is just full of that empty, blissful feeling that you get from having them. That intoxicating high that only a snort will give." He looked at her. "You can run off to Devil, tell him I've got drugs. Probably do me good."

She didn't run off though.

Kneeling down on the other side of the table, she looked at the drugs, then at him. "Do they really help?"

"What do you mean?"

"Does it help you to forget everything and, I don't know, be someone different?"

"You hurt people without guilt and you do shit you'll never remember. They don't help at all, Mandy."

She placed her hand on the table, and he covered

hers with his own. "For a long time, I felt so completely useless and worth nothing that I would find random guys and have sex with them to help me feel anything."

"Is this along with the fights?"

"No, this came after. When I realized there was another way to feel." She had never been open with anyone in her life, not Mia, no one. People always judged who you were by what you did. "I discovered that the thrill of taking a man to a hotel, or a bathroom, or even against a brick wall was much better than trying to get them to hit me. That touching them, using my body to make them want me, that gave me a thrill I didn't even know I was seeking. The feel of their dick as they slid inside me, the risk it took, everything was wrong and so right in the world. I didn't know if I was going to get pregnant or something else. I played Russian roulette with my body." She tilted her head to the side and looked at him.

"Why are you telling me this?"

"You look lost. I … felt it for a long time. That loneliness that consumes you and makes you do things you shouldn't do."

"What happened?" he asked.

"What do you mean?"

"You went from fighting and screwing to cleaning, and living in Piston County. What changed?"

She licked her lips. "One of my ex-partners got in touch with me. He had HIV. He didn't know how long he'd had it or if he'd passed it on to me."

"Fuck," Butler said.

"Yeah, you kind of wake up a little with that. It's not easy to believe that your life could change that fast. I don't have it. I was tested and double-tested. I wanted to make sure they didn't get that wrong. I was clean, and they did test me over a period of time as well. So, I packed my shit up and decided to start living like I care about myself. That's why I clean. It's why I love to work, and why it has been a long time since I've been with a man. Nearly three years now. I've never told another living soul this, ever."

Chapter Four

Butler hadn't been aware of her slide into sexual depravity. That kind of stuff you didn't detect through documents that Whizz could find. Staring across the table, he saw the shock in her eyes at what she'd just told him. Also, he knew she'd shared a part of herself that no one else knew.

"Three years?" he asked.

"Yes."

"Wow. Do you take care of yourself?"

"You mean get myself off?" she asked.

He nodded.

She chuckled. "Yeah, I get myself off. I do what I need to do, and I remember how bad it got." She pointed at his stash. "How bad did it get?"

"I was at the same stage as you. I was with everything. Man, woman, I didn't care. Fucking, snorting, drinking, it was all part and parcel of the life." He told her of his last time, of the oblivion, and his decision to change all that.

"Knowing what you came from, how far you went down, do you even want to consider doing that again?" she asked.

When she put it like that, he felt disgusted with himself. "I didn't touch it."

"I know. It's still tightly sealed."

"I'm surprised you didn't shout for Devil."

"We all go off the rails sometimes, Butler. Some of us it just hits harder than others."

He ran a hand down his face, not really knowing what the fuck to do anymore. Life had gotten so complicated, and it hadn't meant to be. It was supposed to be easy, and yet it felt far from fucking easy. It felt insane, crazy.

"You need to be the one to tell Devil though. You can't keep this secret from him. He'll want to know."

He nodded. "Will you be here when I get back?"

"Yes, I'll stay here. I'll clean your always impeccable room." She smiled, and for a second, he simply watched her. She was such a beautiful woman, and knowing she'd bared her soul to him, it made her even more so in his fucking eyes.

"I'll be right back."

Grabbing the bag, Butler left his room, and made his way toward Devil's office. He checked all around the clubhouse with no sign of him. Heading back upstairs, he found Mandy sitting on his bed.

"No sign of him?" she asked.

"No." He tossed the white bag into his drawer. "I'll tell him later." Closing the door behind him, he took a seat on the bed beside her, not wanting their moment to end. "Thank you."

"For what?"

"For making me see fucking reason. This has been going around my head for fucking days, and I couldn't stop it."

She touched his hand. "Then I'm pleased I opened that door and of course that you didn't lock it."

He locked their fingers together not wanting to let her go. "Three years?"

"Yes, it has been a long time."

"Are you a sex addict?" he asked.

She chuckled. "No. I just … lost it. Nothing made any sense to me, and I didn't want to try. Have I shocked you with my whoring ways?"

"I'm not shocked. Surprised, yes."

He ran his thumb back and forth over her hand. She licked her bottom lip, and the sudden moisture did things to his dick. Her tits seemed to be pressed out, and he couldn't help but reach out, cupping her cheek.

"Butler?"

He didn't speak. Running his thumb across her bottom lip, he pressed it at the midway point and then slowly pushed inside her mouth.

She closed her lips around his thumb and sucked, her tongue stroking over the digit, back and forth. She took it all into her mouth, and he watched, unable to look away.

"What are you thinking about right now?" he asked.

Her eyes had dilated, and her nipples pressed against the front of her shirt. Dropping his hand from her mouth, he stroked her tight bud. She gasped.

"Tell me to stop, Mandy."

She swallowed but didn't say anything to tell him to. Cupping her tit, he turned toward her, but someone knocked at the door, making him pull away with a curse.

Opening the door, he found Sexy waiting there. "Dude, come on, we've got to head out over to Naked Fantasies."

"What the fuck for?" Butler asked.

"Duh, it's on the rotation. Where the fuck is your head? We man the bar and keep an eye on the girls. Devil don't like the fact it was overcrowded the other week, so he's making us deal."

Butler gritted his teeth but nodded. "I'll be there in a minute."

"You okay, man?"

"Yeah, I'm okay. Fuck off." He closed the door, resting against it as he looked at Mandy. She was already on her feet, gathering her stuff.

The moment had been fucking lost, and he hated that.

"I better get cleaning." She moved close to him

and he reached out, cupping her hips and drawing her close.

"I want to know what's going on here."

"Nothing is. I clean for you guys."

"Don't fucking bullshit me right now. I'm not in the mood for it. Something is happening between us. I can feel it, and I know you can."

She sighed and pushed some hair out of her way. He tucked the last strand behind her ear. "This can't happen," she said.

"It's going to."

"I like my job. I love my apartment, and I don't want to do anything to jeopardize that."

"We won't." He gripped the back of her neck, leaning in close, but she put her hands on his chest.

"Not here," she said. "I…"

"Where?" he asked, refusing to back down.

"My apartment later tonight. Not too late."

"I'll be there, Mandy." He released her, opening the door. He grabbed her hand as she was about to leave. "Thank you."

She gave him a nod and walked away.

Grabbing his leather cut, he made his way down toward his bike where Sexy was already straddled on his own bike.

"You got a bitch in your room or something?" Sexy asked.

"None of your business."

"Don't tell me you're about to settle down as well. Our boys are fucking diminishing. I don't think we'll be able to last at this rate."

"You ever think about settling down?" Butler asked.

Sexy burst out laughing. "You've got to be joking, right? Settling down is not on the cards for me. I don't know how you guys can be so pussy-whipped. There's too much to fuck, and I don't want no woman's claim on me. Have you found that woman?"

Butler gave him the finger, and they started their bikes, heading toward the strip club they owned.

He parked up his bike and entered Naked Fantasies. It was already packed for the night, which was fine. He did a quick head count to make sure they weren't over capacity before making his way into the back.

Grabbing the books, he started to look through them. This was all part of the job. He checked the girls' pay, the cost of the booze, and everything seemed in order.

Leaving the office, he locked the door, and made his way around the back where the girls were getting dressed.

He saw a couple of men hanging around, and he urged them out of the way. Sexy was already getting sucked off by one of the women, and Butler wasn't in the mood. Heading back out to the main part of the bar, he sat down at the counter and watched.

His cell phone went off, and he saw it was Devil calling him.

"You at Naked Fantasies?" Devil asked.

"Sitting right here. It's crowded."

"I can see."

"If you can see why do you need us here?"

"Because overcrowding causes a hazard, Butler. It means people will start inspecting, and I don't like nosy bastards in my business. You know this."

"Look, every single night this club is manned by our own."

"Not every single night. We employ a guard on the door some nights, and I have a feeling he's taking money on the side."

Butler closed his eyes and sighed. "Okay, what do you want me to do?"

"Just observe. Listen. I want to know if the other night was just a mistake or if it happens regularly."

"You could just ask the girls," Butler said.

"I don't want to alert them in case they're in on it, Butler."

"I'll report back when I know more."

"Excellent."

****

Mandy paced the length of her apartment. Time was ticking, and she didn't know if she should just go to bed or wait another minute.

Sharing her past with Butler had felt like the right thing to do at the time. Now, she was freaking out because she'd shared a part of herself that she kept private. Running fingers through her hair, she stopped just outside of her bedroom door then paced back to the front door.

"Get a grip, Mandy. This is all good. All fine and good." She glanced down at what she was wearing and winced. She wore a pair of pajama pants and a crop top. She didn't even bother with underwear. "I have to go change."

She took two steps away from the door and there was a knock.

Her heart seemed to kick within her chest, and her hands went all clammy.

Closing her eyes, she counted quickly to three, moved to the door, and checked it was Butler.

He stood on the other side.

One more deep breath and she opened it.

For several seconds neither of them spoke. They just stared at each other.

The tension seemed to mount as the time went by.

Butler didn't say a word. He stepped toward her, and she took a step back. The heat was clear to see in his eyes, and her body went from ice to fire within seconds. Her pussy grew slick, and her nipples hardened.

He closed the door, and they were alone in her apartment.

Swallowing past the lump in her throat, she stared at him, waiting.

He finally caught her arms and pressed her against the door he'd just stepped through.

He took hold of her hands, and pressed them above her head, holding them in place. His commanding presence delighted her.

With both of her hands locked in one of his, he ran the tips of his fingers down her arm, teasing a path toward her breasts.

He slid across one nipple, and she moaned, closing her eyes at the onslaught of immense pleasure from that one touch. He didn't stop.

Butler pinched her nipple, then stroked his finger back and forth. He moved onto her other one, showing it the same kind of attention. Pressing her thighs together, she tried to create some kind of friction, but nothing was relieving the ache that he was building inside her.

She didn't fight against him as his fingers trailed down her chest, going to the edge of her pajama pants as he held her in place.

It had been a long time since she'd felt this kind of arousal, and there was no way she was going to let him stop. Not right now, not ever.

He teased the edge of her pants and she licked her lips, waiting.

Instead of pressing his hand between her thighs, he lifted her shirt up. He made it so that it was covering her head but her body was exposed.

She gasped as he cupped her tit. He held her in his palm, and she couldn't see anything. He kneaded the flesh, and the she felt the wetness of his tongue as he touched her. He slid back and forth across her beaded nipple, and she cried out, the pleasure going straight to her clit.

He sucked on the bud hard, using his teeth to bite down and soothe that pain with his tongue.

She whimpered, not wanting him to stop, just to keep on going.

The pain was almost so much that she nearly screamed for him to stop, but he didn't. He kept on going, only stopping when the pleasure made her ache unbearably.

He moved to the next one, teasing, playing, stroking her body until he'd created a fire within her.

Butler had always intrigued her.

From the moment she started working for Chaos Bleeds MC, he'd captured her attention. She'd done everything in her power to hide it. She never fucked where she worked, even when she spiraled out of control. Bosses, work colleagues, she never slept with any of them. They were always random hookups.

She didn't even think Butler realized she existed, and now his mouth was on her breasts, making her feel so good.

"Hold your shirt," he said.

It was the first time either of them had spoken as he made her hold the shirt. His hand let go of hers, but still, she kept them above her head, not wanting to disappoint him.

He held her hips as he continued to lick and suck at her tits. Over and over he teased her, but he also wasn't in a rush either, taking his sweet time to make her want him more.

"Are you wet for me?" he asked.

"Yes."

He pushed her pajamas down. She felt the band sliding down her thighs until it landed on the floor. She stepped out of them, still keeping the shirt over her face, and her hands above her head.

Butler moaned. "I knew you'd be fucking stunning naked. Your body is made for pleasure."

His hands trailed down to her thighs then up over her stomach, around her back, curving up around her breasts then down again.

Her stomach quivered as he teased just above her pussy.

"You want my hands on you?"

"Yes."

"Oh, Mandy, the things I want to do to you right now."

The promise in his voice couldn't go unheard. She wanted whatever he wanted to dish out. She was his to do with as he pleased.

"Then do it," she said. Her breathing came out in pants. "Do all the things you want to do. I'm not going to fight you." She licked her lips. "I want it."

He tugged the shirt from her body, tearing it in the process. He was still fully dressed, but she didn't care.

Butler slid his hand back between her thighs and began stroking her pussy using two fingers. He teased her clit, putting a finger on either side and gently touching at first. His caress seemed so light that it was next to impossible to get off on it.

When she tried to wriggle on his fingers, he sank them down, plunging deep inside her pussy. She cried out his name, not wanting him to stop. He thrust inside her several times before drawing his fingers back up to stroke over her clit.

"I need to taste you."

His hold was gone, and he pushed her legs apart. Staring down at the floor, she watched him appear. His gaze was on her pussy as he reached out, opening her lips. She closed her eyes as pleasure filled her from his touch alone, but he didn't stop there. His tongue stroked across her clit, light at first as he moved around then down to her entrance and back up again to suck on her clit.

She pressed her hand into a fist. His tongue was driving her crazy but also not allowing her to find that release she so desperately sought.

His hands went from the lips of her pussy to the cheeks of her ass, gripping her tightly as he began to ravish her.

Butler sucked, nipped, licked, and totally took control, driving her crazy with a need that totally blew her away. His tongue was creating all kinds of wickedness, and she felt herself beginning to spiral, to need something to ground her as he took her closer and closer to the edge of her orgasm, controlling her, making her desperate for more.

He was the one that held the control. Only he would choose if she got to come or not. Her orgasm was in his hands, and as he flicked her clit, back and forth, she felt it building. One of his hands left her ass, and he'd held her so tight she knew there would be bruises tomorrow. He plunged two fingers deep inside her, and she cried out, screaming his name as pleasure erupted within her.

Her orgasm took her by such surprise that if he'd not been holding her up as she came, she'd have fallen to the floor.

She'd never come so quickly in all of her life, and even though she'd been with a lot of men, none of them had ever made her come like that.

Butler wasn't finished with her either. Even as she came down from her orgasm, he prolonged her release with gentle strokes and teases on and inside her pussy.

She slapped her hand against the wall, panting as she didn't think she could stand much more.

Only when he was ready did he stop, and as he did, he pulled her down onto his lap, making her wrap her legs around him.

Mandy didn't argue. Holding him tightly, she accepted his kiss as his fingers thrust into her hair.

She tasted herself on his tongue, and she sucked him the instant he plunged into her mouth, moaning.

This was just the start, she felt it.

The line neither of them had crossed before had just been passed.

There was no going back, only forward, and Mandy wasn't afraid of it.

Chapter Five

Butler's cock ached so fucking bad where it pressed against his jeans. It didn't help that Mandy's sweet pussy was riding him. He'd made her come and he felt the damp stain on the fabric, and again he didn't care.

Fucking had to be dirty. There was no room for sweetness and tender loving in what he wanted to do to Mandy.

He wanted to own her, to brand her so that no one else would ever register to her. He wanted her to come to him for all of her sexual pleasure and release. Still with the taste of her on his tongue, he kissed her deeply.

She didn't pull away but seemed to lap that shit up as he claimed her lips. She tasted so good.

He didn't want to stop. Her hands held onto his shoulders tightly as need consumed him.

Mandy began to pull the shirt from him, tugging it off and over his head, letting it fall to the floor. Her hands moved all over his body, leaving a heat that went straight to his cock. He wanted her touch, to feel every part of her all over him, again and again.

"Fuck, baby, you're driving me crazy here. I need more."

He pulled away from the kiss and helped ease her up. Her pussy was directly in front of his face. He couldn't resist pressing a kiss to her lips as he stood up.

Staring into her green eyes, he began to open the belt of his jeans. Her gaze ran down his body, taking every single piece of ink in before resting on his jeans.

He was careful as he pushed it past his aching dick. The last thing he wanted to do was to get that monster stuck in the zipper.

Once his precious dick was all clear, he pushed his jeans down until they landed on the floor, and he kicked them to one side. His boots followed suit, and he finally stood in front of Mandy, the woman he'd been pining for, naked.

Wrapping his fingers around his length, he coated the tip in pre-cum, and slid it all down his length, getting himself nice and slick.

Her tongue peeked out, and he couldn't resist a groan as that made his balls feel heavy.

"You want a taste of my dick?"

"Yes."

He moved toward her, placing his hands on her shoulders as he pushed her down. She didn't fight him, sinking to her knees in front of him. Her breath fanned the length of his cock.

Running his fingers through her long brown strands, he gritted his teeth as her hand finally held his cock.

He wasn't small, and she moved her hands up and down the length, her thumb rubbing against his little slit, which was leaking pre-cum.

With her hair around his fist, he cupped her cheek, tilting her head back.

"Open your mouth."

She slid her lips open, and he pushed the tip between them, watching as they widened to make room for his cock. Her tongue glided along the bottom as he moved in, hitting the back of her mouth before pulling back. A layer of saliva now covered his length. She moved her hand up, working that saliva into his flesh.

As he pushed back into her mouth, she sucked him hard, and he started to thrust. At first, he did so shallowly. He wanted to watch her take him, to take all of him. Her hand would meet to where her lips took, and it still wasn't enough.

When he hit the back of her throat, he didn't

immediately pull away. Slowly, he sank in a little deeper until he hit that gag reflex before he pulled away, but not all the way out. Holding her hair, he moved her face so that he got the perfect angle.

From the fire blazing in her eyes, Mandy fucking loved it. She loved having her control taken away, and he was more than happy to take it. To fuck her into oblivion and to take complete control of her pleasure because he didn't give a shit. He wanted to fuck her, to feel her scream, to hear her erupt, and to take everything that she gave.

He wouldn't hide from that either.

With one hand in her hair, he moved the other around her neck, feeling her pulse against his fingers.

She trusted him.

He saw it in her eyes. As he slid in deep, her mouth opened just a little, and he watched her take him.

When she gagged, he didn't immediately stop this time but allowed her to get accustomed to him. A second later he pulled out until just the tip was there, and he watched her tease the head, swirling her tongue across the head. Pulling out of her mouth, he relished the sight of her licking his dick, tracing across the thick vein up one side and down the other.

Pushing back into her mouth, he went deep, feeling her throat around his tip. She gagged again, but he pushed inside a little more, holding her throat as he did.

Her eyes watered, but she also didn't beg him to stop.

All she had to do was push him away, and he'd release her.

Mandy's hands gripped his thighs. She stroked up to grab his ass, and she actually pulled him in deeper, letting him know she wanted more, that she didn't want him to pull back.

He continued to use her mouth, saliva slick on his cock. Some of it spilled out of her mouth when he didn't allow her to swallow, leaking onto her tits.

Finally, when his balls felt fucking blue and he just couldn't stand it any longer, he moved a little closer, and began to fuck her face, going deep into her throat. He stared at her watching her eyes leak, not with tears but because of her gagging on his cock. Her hands were still gripping his ass so that he knew he'd have bruises from where her nails sank into the flesh, holding him closer.

"I'm going to come in your mouth, and you're not going to swallow straight away. I want to see it, Mandy. See my cum in your mouth, and only when I say you can swallow it, do you."

She nodded her head and gave a moan of consent, which seemed to vibrate up his dick, going straight to his balls.

He fucked her face, loving the way her mouth felt wrapped around his shaft.

Butler had experienced many sleepless nights with this, craving her mouth on him, or her pussy riding his cock.

Nothing had ever seemed to temper his arousal when it came to Mandy. When Devil issued that bullshit rule of not fucking her, Butler had known he was in for a rough time of it. He imagined it was one of the reasons why he'd started to look at Natalie as a way to avoid any temptation.

There was no way he'd have ever been able to have Natalie. He liked her, cared about her, and he thought she was pretty. Not once had he ever wanted to fuck her into oblivion or do what he was doing now, fucking her face as if it was her cunt. As he drove in deep, Mandy gagged around him, and finally relaxed.

Her lips grazed his patch of hair, and it was too much.

He felt his release rush over him.

Pulling out of her throat, as he didn't want her to swallow it straight down, he held the tip at her lips, and watched as his cum filled her mouth with each flowing spurt. He'd not come in such a long time that it seemed to go on forever.

She didn't swallow. His cum was held in a pool in her mouth as he stood back to watch her. He saw everything, and he felt such overwhelming arousal still. There was just something about having his woman naked, kneeling in front of him, with his cum in her mouth.

"Swallow it."

He wrapped his fingers around her throat as he issued the command. Her gaze was on his as her mouth constricted, swallowing it down.

"Show me."

She opened her lips, and it was all gone.

Mandy licked her lips, and he felt the taunt, the tease in her eyes.

"Are you wet for me?"

"Yes."

"Show me."

She dipped her fingers between her pussy, and then held them up.

"No. Lie back, show me what I just did to you, what I made you feel."

Mandy eased back on the carpet, legs spread. She showed her pussy to him, opening her lips, and he saw her wet cunt.

Grabbing one of her chairs he moved it over to where she sat, and he rested his head on his hand.

His cock lay flaccid in his lap, but it wouldn't take long for him to get going again. "Press your fingers into your pussy," he said.

Her fingers moved between her slit, and she teased them inside. He saw a trail of cream leak out of her hole, trailing back to her anus. He'd have that soon. In fact, there wasn't going to be a part of Mandy he didn't have.

He was going to fuck her senseless and make her his.

****

Mandy was so aroused already. She couldn't even believe that she'd already come. Just by having Butler's dick in her mouth, she'd been ready for more. She wanted him inside her. His flaccid cock lay on his leg like a tease to her that she had to wait for him to get back in the game.

Sliding two fingers within her pussy, she watched him. His gaze was on her body. He was just as dirty as she was, and it had been so long since she'd indulged in this that she was desperate for every command and order.

Her body belonged to him as did her pleasure.

It wasn't a Dominant and submissive thing. This was just fucking where he was the one in charge. No rules. Just pure sex.

"Fuck, baby, look at that creamy cunt. You want to be fucked, don't you?" he asked.

"Yes."

"You want my dick inside you?"

"Yes."

"Did you like swallowing my dick?"

"Yes."

He smiled. "How about taking my cum? Did you love the taste?"

Her cheeks heated, and her body was on fire with more. "Yes. I want it again." She saw she'd surprised him. Pulling out of her pussy, she teased her clit, stroking her bud as she watched him.

His hand was on his length. It wasn't hard yet, but she wanted it to be.

"Do you want to possess every single part of me, Butler? To own my mouth." She removed her fingers from her pussy, and she licked her fingers, moaning at her own taste. "You've already taken that."

Sliding her hand down to her tits, she teased the nipples. His gaze was filled with lust, and she loved it. The sight of his arousal was what drove her to keep on going and to not give up this tease. "You want these as well. For me to press them around your cock as you fuck me."

"Yes."

She loved that he wasn't afraid to show his need with her. This was what she wanted. She wanted to be able to be honest with him but to also know everything that he wanted as well. To fuck on equal terms. Down she went, trailing a hand back between her thighs. "You want this pussy?" she asked, turning the questions on him.

"Yes. I hope you're tight for me. I want to feel you wrap around my dick, and I know you're going to struggle to take me."

He was long, and she smiled at his ego.

Her pussy tightened, and she wanted him as well. No doubt about it.

Pushing any of her doubts to one side, she went to her knees, showing him her ass. Spreading her cheeks, she looked over her shoulder at his groan. "You want my ass as well? You want to slide your dick deep in me?"

"Fuck, yes." His cock had started to harden, and she had never been like this with anyone else.

She couldn't even believe she was doing this with Butler. He called to something within her and made her feel safe in his company, knowing he wouldn't hurt her.

Taking a deep breath, she slid her hand across her cheek. Moving between her ass, she stroked from her pussy, getting her fingers slick with her cream as she moved them up to her anus, sliding them across.

"Oh, fuck, Mandy. Yeah, touch yourself. Show me what you like."

She didn't penetrate her ass. She stroked her fingers over her puckered anus, and it did the trick.

Butler moved from the sofa, and he was down on the floor between her thighs. His fingers stroked between her legs, teasing her clit before he drew them back and plunged in deep.

"I'm clean," he said.

"I'm clean, and I'm on the pill."

His fingers were replaced by the tip of his cock. She gasped as he slid the head inside her, filling her with a couple of inches.

He wasn't wrong about his length. It had been so long since she'd been with a man that she was indeed tight and unused to the invasion.

With a couple of inches inside her, he grabbed her hips in a hot, searing grip, and pulled her back. At the same time, he slammed his hips forward and his cock slid right deep inside her, shocking her with how much he filled her. Every single inch stroked within her like a brand that was hot, filled with fire, and she was merely the vessel for it.

They both cried out, the sounds echoing around the walls of the apartment. Her tits felt heavy.

"Weren't expecting that, were you, baby?" He slid his hands over the curve of her ass, spreading her cheeks wide. Both of her hands were now on the floor, holding her steady. "You are a fucking dirty bitch, and I love it, Mandy. I love it, and I that's what I want when you're with me. Don't hold back. I want your dirty, your sweet, your everything."

His hand grabbed her hair. She closed her eyes, panting at the pleasure as he circled it around his wrist. His cock was still buried to the hilt within her. She gasped as he tugged on her hair.

"Damn. We're going to get me some mirrors. I bet you're a sight to behold." With his other hand, he slapped her ass, and she pressed back, wanting more.

His hand landed on her ass again, and she moaned. Her pussy tightened around his length, letting him know how much she was loving his hot touch.

He suddenly began to pull out of her until only the tip of him remained. Butler held himself poised at her entrance, and she panted waiting for him, wanting more. With a hand on her hip and his grip in her hair, she screamed his name as he pounded inside her. Each time the tip of his cock slid inside her, going harder within her.

"Yes, yes, fuck that feels so good," she said.

"You belong to me now, Mandy. You're mine to fuck. No one else. I'll kill any other man that thinks he can touch you. You're mine."

She loved his possession. "There's no one else." She was many things, but she never pitted one man against another. She never allowed anyone to think or believe that there was more between them than what there actually was.

Butler pounded her pussy, and she wished there was a mirror showing her exactly how good his dick looked, all nicely slick and covered in her cream. She was so fucking wet just from thinking it.

"Fuck, baby, what are you thinking?" he asked.

She told him, and he groaned. "We can resolve that."

Mandy whimpered as he pulled out of her.

He released her hair, and he picked her up in his arms as if she weighed nothing. She wrapped her arms around his neck, holding him. She loved it when his arms were around her. She felt safe, comforted. No man had ever left her feeling like that. They normally had the opposite effect on her.

He kicked open the bathroom door, which was one of the only places that held a mirror.

Butler left her stood there, staring at her body. She wasn't perfect. Rounded stomach, cellulite on her thighs, a fuller body, but his touch showed he didn't care about that.

Seconds later he returned with a chair, and the bathroom was big enough for it. He sat down and patted his lap.

She didn't know completely what he had in store for her, but she went with it. He moved her so that she was facing the mirror.

Mandy watched as he held his cock and lowered her down. Watching and feeling it at the same time took her arousal to the next level. His cock sank within her, and she moaned, unable to look away as the lips of her pussy opened up. She saw his cock inside her, her lips open around his length.

Butler moved up so that they were touching, his front to her back, his hands caressing up and down her body. He cupped her tits, pinching the hard nipples before moving down to stroke her pussy, his touch branding her once again.

Using the arms of the chair as leverage, she began to work up and down his length as he teased her clit. Watching his cock slide in and out of her, and his face in the mirror, she knew she wasn't going to last, not now with his gaze on her and seeing his cock.

It was all a sensory overload. Driving down onto his length, she screamed his name as her orgasm took her by surprise. She tightened and pulsed around him. Only when she couldn't take anymore did Butler stop, his fingers moving from between her thighs to hold her hips. He took over, driving her down onto his length at the same time he thrust up inside her, going as deep as he could.

He pounded inside her, the sounds of their moans and slapping flesh filling the room.

Butler groaned, pulled her down hard onto his cock, and she felt him pulse inside her. Wave upon wave of his release flooded her cunt.

When it was over, she leaned back against him, panting for breath. Her eyes closed, basking in what they'd just done.

Butler tapped her thigh. "Watch."

Her gaze went to the mirror, and as he pulled out, she watched his cum leaking from her pussy. He reached between her thighs, and she saw him teasing her with it, pushing it back inside her, and stroking up to her clit.

"I think I've become addicted to you," he said, kissing her neck.

She smiled.

She could live with that.

Chapter Six

A knock at the door made Darcy groan. Rolling onto her side, she saw it was a little after eight in the morning. It was one of the last days in Piston County, and she was so pleased. Yes, she was happy her mom and dad were away and enjoying each other, but she was sixteen years old now. She didn't need a babysitter and could have stayed home in Fort Wills.

"Come in," she said, feeling really tired.

She was always so tired right now. As she ran a hand down her face, the world seemed to be spinning just a little, and she pulled the pillow beneath her as she caught sight of Tabitha entering the room.

"Hey, I hope you don't mind me coming to see you," Tabitha said.

"Nah, it's okay." She was close to Tabitha, even though there was an age gap between them. Where Michael—Alex's son—treated them like a burden, Darcy didn't. She liked hanging out with the other Skulls kids. She was part of it, and they were all a family. In school, no matter what grade they were in, they always had each other's backs, and that was fine with her.

She liked being in a big family.

"I'm surprised you're wasting a second coming to see me. Don't you want to bask in everything that is Simon?"

"He's helping his mom out getting everyone packed up. You've spent most of the trip sleeping. I was worried. Are you dreaming about Ink again? Missing him."

Darcy sighed. She really shouldn't have confessed her feelings for the much older Skulls member. From the first moment she saw him as a prospect she'd had this humiliating crush on him.

"It's fine, honestly."

"Come on, Darcy, you can talk to me."

She reached out, taking Tabitha's hand. "I know I can. It's not like he's ever going to look at me, Tab. You've been very lucky with Simon." Darcy saw a sadness in Tabitha's eyes, and she sighed. "What is it?"

"What if Simon finds someone else? What if there's a girl that is, like, way prettier than me?"

"That's not going to happen."

"How do you know?"

"Because you receive letters every single week, Tab. He loves you, and he's not going to find some replacement girl for you. What if he's worried about a boy?" Darcy asked.

"That's not going to happen, ever. All the boys at school are disgusting and gross. Like Adam. He's always farting, and so are the other boys. Ew." Tabitha stuck her tongue out and did a vomiting noise.

"I'm only saying that he could be worried."

"I know." Tabitha climbed up on the bed, and snuggled in. Darcy didn't have the energy to argue, and she hugged her little friend. "Do you think you can send him a letter?"

"No. It would be lame. He's probably with all the club women right now, anyway." No one knew about her crush with Ink. It wasn't just a crush. She knew that, but everyone would laugh at her anyway.

"You better go."

"Will you be coming out anytime today? It's our last day?"

"I will, Tab. I promise."

Tabitha gave her a hug, and Darcy smiled.

Once the door was closed, she flopped back to the bed. Closing her eyes, she rolled over, snuggling back under the covers. Another few minutes wouldn't hurt.

BUTLER'S WOMAN

****

Butler stared down at the woman in his arms. He waited for the usual panic and fear to set in, but nothing happened. Mandy lay on the bed turned toward him. Her hands were beneath her head, and she looked so happy, so calm, so peaceful. He couldn't believe the dirty words that came out of her mouth last night, or the hot sex they shared.

Reaching out, he teased a strand of her hair back and smiled. She was fucking amazing. Her pussy was so tight, her mouth magical, and just being with her gave him so much pleasure that he couldn't stop thinking about it.

She sighed, moving into his touch. She nuzzled his hand and opened her eyes, smiling.

"Morning," she said.

"Morning to you too."

She yawned and gave a little stretch. "What time is it?"

He glanced at the clock and saw it was a little after eight, and told her so.

"I haven't slept that soundly for a long time."

"I did keep you up half the night."

She turned toward him, chuckling. "That you did." She pulled the blanket up and kept staring at him, her green eyes watching him.

"What?" he asked.

"I was just wondering what the protocol is?"

"What do you mean?"

"Well, I don't know what to do. I've never done the morning-after thing."

"You've not had a man in your bed?"

"Nope. I always avoided the next day thing in case it was awkward. It was just a random hookup with the guys. I didn't want to know their number."

"I can tell you that it's too late for that with me."

"Why?"

"I already programed my number into your cell. You've got me."

She groaned, but he saw the smile on her lips. "So, this is not a casual hookup?"

"No, it's not. I meant what I said, Mandy. No other men. Only me."

"If that's the case then you cannot touch any of those club women either. If I can't have another man, neither can you have another woman."

"That's fine by me. I've not been with any of those women in a long time."

"A long time?" she asked.

"Yes. Roughly around the time that the club got a new cleaner. I don't know if you know her. She has green eyes, brown hair, sexy as fuck. I loved her ass when she'd be cleaning under tables."

She chuckled, and damn it, that sound went straight to his dick.

"Wow, she sounds pretty special."

"She is. Not when she's banging her head though and making me worry. Kind of made me feel guilty for just staring at her ass and thinking about how she'd react if I slid in deep within her cunt."

She sighed. "That's so romantic."

The sound of his stomach growling filled the air, and they both chuckled. "How about I go and make us something to eat?"

"You can cook?"

"Yes, and I would very much like to cook for you."

"Then I'm more than happy for you to do that."

He reached out, stroking her cheek. Running his thumb across her bottom lip, he tilted her head back and claimed her lips. She moaned, and he plunged his tongue in her mouth. Her hands went to his shoulders, and he pressed her against the bed.

Suddenly pulling away, he smiled down at her. "Food first."

"We can do something else."

"I know you're only after my body, but I want you full so that when we do fuck again, I don't have to stop. I've got to keep you healthy." He kissed her again and climbed out of bed.

He walked toward the door, and she laughed. "You're going to cook breakfast naked?"

"No. I'm going to wear an apron." He winked at her. "Oh, my rules, and you *are* to come to the table completely naked. No clothes until we leave the apartment." He winked at her, and she chuckled.

Entering the kitchen, he found an apron and quickly pulled it on. Opening her fridge, he grabbed some eggs and bacon. It didn't take him long to find everything he needed as he started up breakfast.

He was cracking eggs when her head popped around the corner of the wall.

Butler chuckled. "Have you gone shy on me?"

"I think I have."

"You've not walked around this place butt ass naked?"

"No. It's not something I've thought about. When I get home, I eat, shower, and crash. Don't really have time to linger."

"Well, strut your stuff. Show me how a woman works her place."

She rolled her eyes, and he simply waited.

Mandy stepped out from behind the wall, and the sight before him was truly spectacular just as he knew it would be.

Her tits were high and tipped with beautiful, large red nipples. She was all curves and softness. His cock woke up instantly, and he wanted her. The sizzling of the bacon distracted him.

"Go on, baby, walk around."

"Seriously?"

"This is your place. Own it."

Turning the bacon, he whisked the eggs and watched as she moved around the room. She began to put a few things away. A couple of books were open on the coffee table, and she closed them. Their clothes, piled on the floor, she folded neatly.

"You never stop cleaning, do you?"

"I don't like a lot of mess. I know. It's my job to clean, but it's more than that. I can't think in mess. It's gross, and I don't live with gross." She looked around the sitting room before walking back to the kitchen. Even as he cooked breakfast, she avoided the stove but cleaned around him.

Every now and then her tits brushed against his back or some other part of her did, and it made him ache to be inside her.

Within minutes he had the breakfast cooked and they were sitting at her small dining room table. She'd put some towels on the seats, which he did find utterly adorable.

"This is really good."

"Cooking helped me to focus while I was getting clean."

"It did?"

"Yeah, reading a cookbook, following everything exactly, it helped. I did it in rehab, and for a little while when I got back, but then life didn't always allow for an exact routine."

"Do you like club life?"

"What do you mean?"

"Well, the way you're talking about it, you don't seem happy."

"Oh, I am. It's complicated."

"I'm a good listener," she said. "Unless you don't feel comfortable talking about it. I know the club has a lot of secrets."

He sighed. "For a long time, we've had a lot of bad shit happening. Bad guys from the past, present, and I tell you it felt like the fucking future. We lost men and women from both of our clubs. It was a nightmare. I had to constantly sleep with one eye open. The club needed me, and I was finally clean. I could hold my own, and they didn't have to worry about me being a weak link."

"That's important to you?"

"Yes. Being in Chaos Bleeds, it's been everything. I didn't have a lot in life. No family, friends, no job. My entire existence has been about serving in the club, and it's what I'm good at. It's what I know and what I love."

"Okay."

"Now, we're taking a different path. One that comes away from all the trouble. For the first time since I've been clean, I've not been distracted."

"And temptation is there?"

"It's always been there, you know, I just didn't realize how much."

"Do you think you can live without it?" she asked.

"I know I can. I just..." he stopped running a hand down his face. "I'm disappointed in myself, Mandy. That's what I am. I caved, and now I have some stash that I've got to talk to Devil about. It's ... it's bullshit. That chapter of my life, it was over. I don't want to lose my club over this."

"Do you think you will?" she asked.

"I don't know. I know I've got to talk to him."

"Would you like me to come with you?"

"No, this is something I've got to do on my own, no matter how much I hate it. It's a weakness, and he needs to know."

She reached out, touching his hand. "I think you're a very brave person."

"I'm not brave."

"You didn't take it. You didn't cave to that need. You just … you stopped. I'm here, Butler. If you ever need me, I'm here."

"Thank you, baby," he said.

He squeezed her hand, and they enjoyed their breakfast. All he wanted to do was spend the day with her, but he didn't have a choice. He had to go back to the clubhouse and deal with his problem.

It was driving him crazy knowing it was there. After breakfast, he waited for Mandy to get dressed. He was dropping her off in town to grab some supplies. While she was busy, he intended to talk to Devil, to get it all out in the open with him.

Butler knew if he went down that road of drugs again, he wouldn't ever recover. It was why he'd cut it all out, drugs and booze. He didn't even take a painkiller for a headache anymore.

He didn't want to lose that kind of control, and now with Mandy, he didn't know what the fuck that was but it meant something to him. He wouldn't lose that. He couldn't.

****

Piston County was a small town. When Mandy first arrived, she'd found it quite charming. Like all places it had good and bad areas. Most of her life she'd been around the bad areas. Lexie and Devil's place though, that was from the good area. Standing outside Lexie's home, Mandy raised her hand, and gave a knock. She heard a lot of commotion inside, and Simon was the one to open the door. She'd gotten a call from Lexie asking if she could bring some bags to her home. Seeing no reason not to, after she got her groceries, she had picked up what Lexie needed and took a cab home. After putting away her stuff, she drove back toward Lexie's home.

She'd left a few texts for Butler, but she had yet to hear from him. It had only been an hour and half, but she was worried. How long did it take to talk to Devil?

"Hey, Mandy," Simon said, opening the door.

He looked utterly miserable.

"What's wrong?" she asked.

"Oh, don't mind him," Lexie said, coming toward her. She took the bag that was offered to her. "He's miserable because this is Tabby's last day here, and he doesn't want her to leave."

"It's an entire summer. She doesn't have to go."

"I know. I know." Lexie kissed his head.

Simon tutted and walked away.

"He's growing up so fast. Thank you so much for bringing me this. You want a cup of coffee?"

"I'd love some." She shoved her hands in her pockets following Lexie back toward the kitchen. "Have you heard from Devil or Butler?"

"No, not since Devil left this morning. He did mention something about needing to talk to one of the girls at Naked Fantasies, but that's about it."

Mandy winced, hating the thought of Butler near any woman who was half-naked. "How do you handle that?"

"Handle what?" Lexie asked.

"You know. Strippers. Naked Fantasies. Lots of

semi-clad women walking around."

Lexie laughed. "I don't worry about it."

"How can you not?" Already she was worried that another woman could have eyes on Butler, and she was possessive. Butler belonged to her, and she didn't want to share him with anyone.

"It's simple. I know I keep my man satisfied and he'd never stray."

"You're really convinced of that?"

"I know Devil, and believe me, he won't stray."

"That must be nice." She bit her lip, thinking of all the men her mom had a relationship with.

"I love him, and he loves me. We've been through a lot together. Devil wouldn't throw that all away for a casual hookup. I trust him." Lexie placed a hand on her arm. "Did something happen with you and Butler?"

"I don't know what it is or anything. He won't get into trouble, will he?"

"No, he's a grown man."

Lexie placed a cup of coffee in front of her. She lifted it and took a sip.

"Thank you for getting these. Everything is so hectic today. They've all bought new clothes, and of course they have to go in the suitcases, and all the old ones are going in the bag, and I didn't have time to go get them."

"It's fine. I was at the grocery story anyway."

Eva walked into the kitchen with a sigh. "You know, I hate packing." She flopped down in her seat, running fingers through her hair. "Next time we come here, I'm coming on my own. Minus the kids."

Lexie laughed and seconds later put a coffee in front of her. "Why did you agree to take all of the kids?"

"Lacey and Whizz needed to get away. It had

been a long time since they had a vacation, and then of course Murphy and Tate wanted some time alone. It just made sense. Lash and Angel are away as well. Thank you for letting us stay here for a couple of days."

"Even though Devil pretends to hate it, he loves this house filled to bursting with kids," Lexie said.

"I don't remember your name," Eva said, looking at her.

Mandy chuckled. "I'm Mandy. I clean a lot."

"I'm Eva, but from the look on your face you remembered my name."

"I did, yes, but don't worry about it. With how many kids are around, I was shocked when Butler handled them all the other day."

"Yes, they all said how much fun they had," Eva said. "It doesn't always happen like this, but between the two clubs, we like to have some time over breaks."

"What she is really trying to say is our kids pretty much order us around. They're best friends, and of course that means they have to be together during breaks." Lexie shrugged. "It's not hard, but it means Thanksgiving this year is totally at The Skulls."

"Angel will cook. It'll be awesome."

She listened as the two women began to organize the upcoming holidays, and she smiled through it. When kids began to invade the kitchen, Mandy made her excuses and left the house. Climbing into the car, she drove back home, and checked her cell phone. Still nothing from Butler.

Come on, Butler, tell me you're all right.

Chapter Seven

Butler sat in front of a now-sobbing Louise as she cried out the story of her pimp wanting an in at Naked Fantasies. She had to get the job and get the girls on her side, and then bring in the drugs.

So not only was Naked Fantasies becoming overcrowded, but there was now a drug problem as well. Out of the twenty girls that worked there, all different shifts, different weeks and nights, there were ten who were now hooked on heroin. Not only that, they had a pimp to find and deal with.

"I'm so sorry, Devil. I didn't want—"

"Shut the fuck up. You were never one of the girls in the club. You were given a job, and you abused your position. You're fucking useless." Devil paced the length of the club, which was closed.

Vincent was standing there, arms folded, and angry. They all were.

With the girls now hooked on the drugs, Devil had no choice but to cut them loose, even if he did send them to rehab.

The moment he entered the clubhouse today, Devil had told him they had work to do and that they could talk later about whatever it was he wanted. He couldn't believe this was right in front of him, and it pissed him the fuck off that he'd been too distracted to see it.

"We need the pimp," Vincent said.

"Yeah, we fucking do."

"I can't tell you. He'll kill me."

Since Devil had been with Lexie, he'd been more lethal but also considerate to women who stripped. There was a time he'd seen them all as whores and easy women. Seeing as Lexie got dumped with Simon from her sister, she'd had no choice but to strip to make some decent cash to take care of him.

They all adored Lexie. It took a special and strong kind of woman to not only love a child that wasn't your own but to make those kinds of sacrifices. They were all sworn to secrecy. Simon would never find out the truth about any of what happened. Devil asked it of all of them to forget the truth.

Lexie's commitment to Devil and the club was one of the reasons why Butler got clean. He wanted to protect the club and their women at all costs.

Any compassion Devil had was wiped out with Louise. He pulled out his gun, and grabbed her head, pulling it back and pressing the tip against her temple. "Do you really fucking think right now you need to worry about your piece of shit pimp? You think you're going to walk away free of all this?"

"You don't hurt women," Louise said. "He said so. My man said so."

Devil smiled. "You really think that? I've killed women who have done less wrong than you."

There was only one woman that Devil allowed to get away with hurting him, and that had been Kayla. The woman who gave birth to Simon, the woman who was Lexie's sister. She had been killed by one of the club's enemies.

He put his gun away, and Sexy passed him the knife. "I think we'll start first with fucking up this face. No one will want to pay you shit with a face that shrivels their dick."

Butler waited for the woman to crack, and within seconds she did, screaming the name and location of the pimp. It was a surprise to learn that the pimp in question lived a few houses away from Devil.

"Excellent. Call him," Devil said. "We need to

have a little chat."

They waited as Louise grabbed her cell phone. The threat was still there, so she asked for her pimp to come down. She even made up a lie about one of the girls needing a hit.

Ripper and Dick were watching the girls in the back. The ones that hadn't succumbed to the drugs had been allowed to leave. Of course, they all had to piss in a cup for the test to be complete, and Jessica hadn't loved being involved in that.

She was taking her maternity leave really seriously and didn't like being pulled away from her daughter.

Butler's cell phone buzzed in his pocket, but he didn't want to be distracted even as he wanted to see if Mandy was okay.

Devil walked over to them as Sexy and Guts guarded Louise.

"I can't kill her, but there's no way I'm allowing her to leave her without any consequences," Devil said. "Neither can her pimp."

"What do you want to do?"

"We need Lola on this pronto. Whizz is away, and he tends to work faster in situations like this. She needs to find out everything she can about them. I want to know every single detail before I hand them over. Michael can deal with them, but I want to know everything first."

Sinner was already there, putting the call through to his wife.

"You okay?" Butler asked.

"No, I'm not. I knew something was off, but I didn't know what. The fact we hired a whore with a pimp wanting access pisses me off. What happened to each person being checked on?" Devil asked.

"We made a few mistakes," Vincent said. "I wouldn't worry too much."

"With our track record, I'm not going to let this slide."

If they did, it could mean bad news for the club. They had a bad reputation, which kept a lot of people off their turf and they liked that, needed it even. The last thing they wanted was someone trying to ruin the club or take over in Piston County. It would mean an all-out war, and, seeing as they acted as a form of safe house for people in need of help, that wouldn't work.

"I'm going to have to make an example of this situation. I'm going to make sure that Michael completely wipes out this entire fucking problem so they know that Chaos Bleeds is not to be messed with."

"We can't kill her?" Butler asked. "It has been a long time since I actually dug a grave." He stared at his hands. "They'll blister, but they'll heal."

"I can't. New rules state that dead bodies can't just magically disappear or start piling up."

"You sure you really need to call Michael? A couple dead bodies won't be a problem."

Michael Granito was the man responsible for approaching The Skulls and asking for their help. Chaos Bleeds had also taken on the deal as well and would act as a backup to The Skulls.

"Yes, I gave my word, and this is not just a slight against the club. This is drugs," Devil said.

"Anyone remember when we could just kill and be done with it?" Curse asked. "You know, the good old days."

"Yeah, well, these are the sacrifices we have to make in order to get this shit to work." Devil sighed. "I hate talking to Michael."

He didn't like having to deal with anyone else.

"It's your call," Butler said. "We're all happy for you to put them in the ground. No one here will talk."

Devil glanced back at the woman then looked around the club. "Drugs."

"What?" Vincent asked.

"The drugs. Take the pimp and the whore out of the equation, we've got a drug problem."

Butler frowned. "So?"

"I've got to call Michael. He can identify the drugs and find the source. This pimp may not be a supplier but a distributor. Our girls are hooked, but I want to know where it's coming from. Naked Fantasies needs to be closed until further notice. The women that didn't use, we're going to have to put them on half pay until we can get enough women to strip."

Already shit was hitting the fan, and as he watched Devil, Butler knew he had to come clean. Drugs were a problem, and no matter how much he hated it, he had to tell him.

Thinking about the packet of white powder in his room, Butler called to Devil.

"I told you, we'll talk as soon as we handle it."

"No, I need to talk now." Part of the deal with Michael was that they all stayed clean. He was clean, but right now he had evidence to suggest otherwise.

"I've got a bigger problem than you banging the cleaning lady."

"I've got drugs at the clubhouse," Butler said. He'd not wanted to come out like this in front of most of the men.

He felt their gazes on him as Devil stopped and turned to look at him.

Sick to his stomach, he stared at his club Prez, who stepped close to him.

"What the fuck are you saying?" Devil asked.

"I didn't take it. It's all there, but … I wanted to. Mandy can tell you. She was there."

Devil ran a hand down his face. "Get the fuck out of my face."

"Devil—"

"I am trying to make everything fucking work in this new world we're living in. One where we stay the fuck out of trouble and our men don't die. You're telling me that life has gotten a bit too cushy for you and that you can't handle it?"

Guilt filled him as he stared at his club Prez.

"I wasn't thinking."

"No, you fucking weren't, which is the problem with all addicts. They're selfish little cunts who only see themselves. Get the fuck out of my club right now. I swear, Butler, right now. I had you taking care of my kids, looking after my woman. Get out of my fucking sight."

Butler didn't argue. When Devil spoke, everyone had no choice but to listen, and leaving the bar, he went to his bike.

He held onto the seat, clenching his hands into fists, and yelled as he shoved his bike over.

Angry at himself at his weakness he just erupted, growling in rage. He slammed his fist against the brick wall. The pain did nothing to lessen his disgust at himself.

He slammed both of his fists against the wall, and suddenly he stopped. Blood on his knuckles, pain across his hands and up his arms, he leaned forward, and panted.

"You okay?" Dick asked.

Butler looked up, surprised to see Dick there. He was one of the people who had gone to rehab, who'd fought it with him.

"You here to gloat?"

"Nope. If you're hoping to take out that wall, you don't have super strength."

"I'm not interested in listening to this shit right now, Dick." Butler panted, trying to get himself back under control.

"I know what it's like."

He stopped and looked up at his club brother. "When everything settles down and you take a moment, you think about what you've done and you realize that you need it. You crave that high more than anything else in the world because part of you is afraid to enjoy this peace, this silence."

"You ever go back?" Butler asked. "You ever been tempted?"

"Tempted, yes. I've never gone and bought it though. I've got my kid, my woman. I can't go back to that life. I do that, I want Devil to put a bullet through my head. He's agreed to do it as well."

"You won't fight it?"

"I'm fighting it now, but I won't put my woman through that shit. She had to with her sister." Dick stepped forward. "That's how I met her, you know. Martha. At the rehab center. She was there with her sister. The drugs kept her sister down to the point that Martha was in an accident and because she was impaled by a fucking tree, she had to listen to her sister choke on her own vomit."

Butler liked Martha. Anyone who could put up with Dick's dickish ways was a good woman as far as Butler was concerned.

"Which is why if I touch any of it, I'm a dead man. Devil promised me, and we all know he keeps them fuckers."

Butler smiled. "What are you trying to say to

me?"

"Simple. You don't want to start up again. I know you don't because you're like me. This club is your life. Hang onto that feeling and while you're at it, why don't you focus all that obsession on your woman? You'll be surprised how little the drugs mean to you then."

****

Mandy sat curled up on her sofa. Her cell phone lay on the table, and she kept on waiting for it to go off. It was nearly seven now, and she was going out of her mind. Biting her thumb, she jumped as there was a knock on the door.

Rushing toward the door, she saw it was Devil, and she frowned. He was alone, and her heart started to race.

"I know you're in there, Mandy. Don't even think to try and push me right now. I'm not in the fucking mood."

Closing her eyes, she rested her head against the door, and seeing no other alternative, she opened it.

He looked … pissed.

Moving away from the door, she went back to sitting on the sofa, waiting as Devil closed the door, and entered the room.

"I take it you know why I'm here?"

"I don't really know why you're here, and I don't want to try to guess," she said.

"Butler, a nice white little bag of powder. Ring any bells?"

"Is he alive?" she asked.

"Of course he's alive. I'm about to go and see him, but before I beat the fucking living shit out of him, I figured I'd come and talk to you, seeing as you saw him."

She ran fingers through her hair. "He was staring

at it. I know I should have shouted for you, but he looked so lost and I didn't want to get him into trouble."

"You should have shouted for me." Devil leaned back in his seat. "You know you were supposed to help matters, not make them worse."

"What?"

"I saw the way he looked at you. I knew he wanted you. I knew you liked him even though you hid it. It was the covert looks you gave him. Every time he came into a room, you'd always turn toward him, watching him."

"How did you know?"

"I know everything, Mandy. It's why I accepted you back, and why I made sure there was a thorough background check on you. I know my men. I know what they need, and you'll be good for Butler. You'll keep him focused." Devil leaned forward. "I always knew it was a risk with the men who used. Addicts aren't the most reliable, you know."

"I don't."

"Well, the ones willing to stick around, I knew I'd do whatever I could to help them."

"And those that didn't?"

"They're not around anymore, Mandy. I need to know that you're in this."

"What?"

"Don't even pretend to not understand what I fucking mean about this. You know what I mean and what I want. Are you serious about Butler or are you just playing him?"

"If you're asking for forever I don't know. You can't know that he wants that."

"I know that you're the first woman to get through to him, and that means something to me. He tries around you, and that's what I need. What I want to know from you is if you're ready for that kind of commitment. I need to know."

She licked her dry lips. "I'm … yes." She pushed all of her fear aside and focused on the man in front of her.

"I know this is asking for a lot and that you don't have a good track record with all of this."

"When it comes to Butler, I want to help. I want to do whatever you need me to do in order to make this work."

"Good."

Devil got up, and she frowned, looking toward him.

"Where are you going?"

"I'm going to deal with Butler. No, I'm not going to kill him. At the moment my need to kill has been pushed to one side, all for the matter of business." Devil stood, and he looked at her.

The look scared the shit out of her.

"My men mean the world to me, Mandy. I don't take them being hurt lightly."

"I won't hurt him."

"Good. He should be back to you in one piece."

She watched him leave.

The threat was clearly there. She didn't have a clue what she'd just done or what she'd signed up for.

****

Devil slammed his office door closed and Butler stood, watching his Prez.

"Dick told me what you did to your hands."

He stared down at them. They were cut up and swelling.

"Did you break anything?" Devil asked.

"No. Devil, I'm sorry."

"I don't want to hear you're sorry. I want the

drugs now."

Butler pointed at the desk. "I already got it. I figured you'd want it."

Devil picked up the bag and sighed. "This looks like the same stuff the girls had in the club."

"I wasn't thinking."

"Yeah, well, it just so happens that Michael knows the team that is currently hunting the pipeline of this drug. The girls at the club have been lucky. A lot of people have died from taking this. It's bad stuff."

"Shit," Butler said.

"Yeah, they're mixing it with poisons and shit."

"What happened to the pimp?"

"He's now in the tender loving care of the Feds, and I don't give a shit." Devil sat back in his office chair. "Until further notice the club is closed. The miserable men of Piston County won't have any bare tits to drool over."

"Can't you keep it open?"

"Not with half the girls fired and heading to rehab. Michael is questioning them all. You were to come to me with this."

"I know."

"I need to know when you're about to fall off the wagon, or if you're having doubts about your place in the club."

"I don't have doubts."

Devil sat forward. "This new era within the club, it's going to have its problems. Ups and downs, left and right. That kind of thing. I want you to take some time."

"What? You want my patch?"

"Yeah, I do. I want your patch, and I want you to take some time away from the club."

"Devil?"

"Hear me the fuck out. Nothing serious is going

down right now. The club is closed for the time being, but I want it dealt with pronto. I'm dealing with Michael. He's an asshole, but he gets it, okay? We're not in a bad place, but I need to know you're serious about this. I can't have this. Dick took some time. Men take time, Butler, and you haven't. We've dealt with shit after shit, and still you've come back fighting. This, though, this is the final straw." He held up the white packet. "This club is not just about the men riding for kicks. It's about a lot more than that, and I need to know you're with it. We're all changing, and as much as I'd love to hand you in to Michael, I know I owe you more than that. The club owes you this chance. It'll be the only one you get."

"I'm here. I swear." Giving up his patch was like tearing out a part of his soul. "I can't…"

"This is not me asking you, Butler. This is me telling you. Give me your fucking patch now." Devil spoke slowly, calmly, and as Butler removed his leather cut, he held it hard in his fist.

This was fucking cutting him to the core, killing him inside.

He reached out and placed it in Devil's hand.

"Now, I want you to take some time. A week or two, or even longer if you need it."

"What do you want me to do?"

"I want you to think about the club, your place in it, and what we're going to be doing. Take a good, long think about it because this is not happening. Not anymore. We don't have time for error or falling off the wagon to get back up. We're not a bunch of men riding around causing fights and having fun. Piston County is our home. It's our turf. I've got a wife and kids. We have a lot more to protect now than we ever have before. You all voted for this, but I understand if it's too much, and you can go." Devil folded up his leather cut, and Butler watched as it was placed in the safe. "You call me and we'll talk whenever you want. Just take some time. Find who you are, and know that I need the Butler that came to me after rehab. That's who I need in my club. Not someone who is going to fall."

Butler nodded and got up.

He didn't need Devil to tell him the conversation was terminated.

He had to get his patch back, but he also had to do what his Prez felt was right.

Chapter Eight

Pacing nervously back and forth across her room, Mandy kept going to the door and stopping. What the hell was going on? She was freaking out, and it was all because of the visit from Devil. The last thing she wanted was for Butler to get in trouble because he didn't do anything wrong. Not a damn thing, and she was scared for him, terrified.

She'd watched him for some time now and knew without a doubt that the club meant everything to him.

Another knock on her door made her jump. Feeling like absolute crap, she went and opened the door without even checking to see who it was. Butler stood on the other side of the door. He wasn't wearing his leather cut.

The moment she stared into his eyes, she saw the pain but also the instant shot of lust that stared back at her.

She took a step back, and he entered her home.

Once again, neither of them said a word as he closed and locked the door. Her pussy clenched at the promise in his eyes.

The moment the lock clicked in place it seemed to echo around the room.

Butler stepped right up to her.

No words as he sank his fingers into her hair, pulling her close. His rough handling turned her on. Pressing her hands to his chest, she stared up at him, waiting.

"Right now, I want to fuck us both into oblivion. Tell me if you can't handle that because I want to use you, Mandy. I want to fuck you with everything that I've got and then take some more."

"Then take it, Butler," she said. "I'm not made

out of glass. I can take whatever you've got to throw at me."

She gasped as he pushed her against the wall. He grabbed her hands and held them in place as his lips took possession of hers. This wasn't gentle; far from it.

He bit her bottom lip, sucking it between his teeth before letting her go. His lips trailed down her neck, sucking on the pulse. His teeth grazed her flesh. Closing her eyes, she basked in his touch, wanting more, not wanting him to stop, not for a single second. She wanted his touch, his control, to be completely consumed by him.

"Don't fucking move them," he said, releasing her hands.

She stayed perfectly still as he grabbed the edge of her shirt and pulled it off. Next, he dealt with her jeans, and she kept her arms up in the same place as piece by piece he removed her clothing.

She whimpered, moaned, gasped, and was completely taken over as his hands and lips trailed down her body. His hands moved all over, consuming her with fire.

He slipped his hand between her thighs and chuckled. "So fucking wet for me. I find that incredibly hot, baby." Two fingers slid in deep, and she moaned, thrusting down onto them, wanting them inside her. He stretched her with a third finger, but didn't keep them in her for long before he pulled them back and stroked her clit.

Fire built within her as he teased her pussy.

At the same time, his lips attacked her nipples, biting at the beaded tips, sucking on each one.

He pulled his hand from her pussy to press her tits together, his tongue flicking across each bud.

Suddenly, his touch wasn't on her anymore, and

she panted, waiting for more.

Butler stepped back, his hands going to his belt as he removed the long loop. He pushed them down, and his cock sprang forward.

He was long and thick. Her pussy tightened recalling how good he felt inside her, and she wanted him again. He pulled his shirt off, and then he was on her.

His lips ravished her mouth as they moved back into her sitting room. Butler sat down on the chair, and with a tug of her hands, she fell on him. He moved her so that she straddled his lap. The tip of his cock was pointing up. He guided her over his dick, and as she sank slowly down onto his length, he released a groan that only made her want more.

Inch by inch, he filled her. His hands went to her hips, and he pulled her down, slamming up inside her those last few, making her cry out.

Gripping his shoulders, she panted as the depth of him was between pleasure and pain, at the fine line that blurred between.

She licked her dry lips, staring at him.

His cock pulsed within her, and her pussy clenched around him.

"We fit fucking perfectly. Do you feel it, baby? How good we are together?"

"Yes."

His hands moved from her hips, sliding up to cup her tits. His thumbs ran back and forth across her nipples, which were so sensitive that the smallest touch set her off.

"I've spent a lot of time thinking about fucking you, and I'm going to use your body exactly how I've been wanting it. Understand?"

"Yes."

"I hope you can handle it."

He lifted her up off his cock so that only the tip was inside her before slamming her back down. For several thrusts he did this, jarring her with the force of each one. He wasn't gentle. This was about ownership.

Butler was taking ownership of her body, and she wasn't putting up a single fight because she didn't want to.

Her body belonged to him right now, and she'd do everything he asked, no matter how uncomfortable it was.

She held onto his shoulders, feeling every inch as it hit right in deep, bumping her cervix, but that wasn't enough for Butler.

He changed positions, making her kneel on the edge of the sofa as he stood behind her.

He slid in deep as his hands went to her hair, using his grip to fuck her hard. Her tits rubbed against the edge of the sofa. He slapped her ass, using her body, but again it wasn't enough.

This time he moved her into the bedroom. He pressed her down onto the bed and settled between her thighs.

He lifted her legs up, so that they were open wide as he slid inside her.

His was gaze on her, and she couldn't look away even if she wanted to. With the way he was working her body, she felt him right down deep in her soul, and it struck her that he'd chosen a position that made her see him, that made her think of all the times she'd watched him.

Right now, as he fucked her hard, he held her in place, and she recalled his smile. The way he looked when he was happy, and the yearning she felt to be with him, to know him, to be part of everything with him.

She'd never told anyone that she had the biggest crush on this man. Why would she? She wasn't a teenager anymore and didn't need to go spilling all of her secrets to her friends.

He released her legs and grabbed her hands, holding them to the bed, his lips taking hers once again as he drove inside her.

His cock was so slick that she heard the wetness as he plunged within her pussy.

She gripped his hands tightly, not wanting this moment to end as he filled her. Something was changing between them. Whatever had happened, it was like Butler had made the decision of what he was going to do next, and she didn't have much choice in the matter, not that she needed one.

He pistoned inside her, the bed rocking, hitting the wall as he did.

Butler came with a groan, shocking her a little that he'd come without her finding any release, not that she minded one bit. She'd had plenty of sex where her needs were not met. She just didn't expect it of Butler.

The moment his release was done, he pulled out of her and slid to the side. She was about to leave, to roll off the bed, and go to the bathroom.

Butler's hand on her thigh kept her still.

"I needed that, but don't think for a second that I would ever allow you to be unsatisfied." He cupped her pussy, and even though he'd finished inside her, he slid two fingers in and pulled them back, stroking over her slit.

Pleasure rushed through every single part of her, shocking her at the intensity. Two fingers stroked on either side of her nub. She was so sensitive that his touch seemed way too much, but he stroked across, over, on either side before sliding down, fucking her cunt, before teasing her clit. At the same time, he sucked her nipple into his mouth, and she whimpered.

Her orgasm was fast approaching, and Butler seemed intent on wanting to prolong that.

He teased her until she couldn't take it anymore, and he relented. When she finally reached her climax, she screamed his name.

****

Butler removed his cum-soaked fingers from her pussy when he was satisfied that her orgasm had finished. He didn't like his woman to go without, and Mandy belonged to him. She may not like it at the moment, but that didn't matter to him. She was his woman, and he intended to take care of all of her needs.

He pressed his fingers to her mouth, and Mandy sucked them clean, tasting them both on them. Once he was clean, he pulled her into his arms, kissing the top of her head.

"What happened?" Mandy said. "I know you came in, and we fucked, but you've got to tell me what Devil said."

"He took my cut."

"What? Does this mean you're no longer part of the MC?"

"No. I've got to take time to know what I want. He doesn't have time for people who go out and buy drugs because they're feeling bored."

She tilted her head back, and the moment he stared into her green eyes, he felt like he could focus again. "You were bored?"

"Up until that point my thoughts had been focused on everything else. The club, the enemies, helping everyone to stay alive." He sighed. "I fucked up big time."

She placed a hand on his chest and rubbed back

and forth. He liked that she wanted to comfort him.

"Devil came here. I told him that you didn't take those drugs."

"He believes you, Mandy."

"Then why would he do this?"

He pushed some of her hair off her face, stroking her cheek. "Because we've got a deal with someone that means we have to stay out of trouble. Possessing drugs is the very opposite of that."

"But ... it was a mistake."

"Some mistakes can't be taken back." He gritted his teeth, angry with himself. Trailing a finger down her body, he teased across her puckered nipple. "I've got no place to stay, so I was wondering if I could crash here for a bit."

"Of course. You lived at the clubhouse?"

"Yes. There was never any reason for me to find a place of my own."

"You can stay here as long as you want."

"You ever had a boyfriend stay with you?" he asked.

"Is that what you are now, my boyfriend?"

"Yes. You're mine, Mandy."

"You'll be the first man to ever live with me."

"I feel honored."

She chuckled. "You've not lived with me long enough to know if you want to be honored by that role."

"Believe me, I do. Also, I'm going to be coming with you on jobs."

"Really? You want to come and help me clean?" she asked.

"Why not? It'll do me good. I can clean, and I can take orders. So long as you understand that you follow mine the moment we're together here. When it comes to sex, what I say stands."

"I think I can live with that." She placed a hand on his body. "Are you sure you're doing the right thing?"

"I've got no choice. I've never seen Devil like that. At least not to one of his men. I've got to prove to him I want this."

"How?"

"He doesn't have the time for someone who's more interested in buying drugs than protecting the club. This is my mistake. I completely screwed up. I'll make it right. I have to."

She looked worried, and he held her tightly.

"What's wrong?" he asked.

"I'm just … I was so scared for you. Waiting to see what would happen. When Devil came here, I didn't know what to expect."

"You thought he'd killed me?"

"I don't know. It's all so new, you know?"

He smiled. "I know, and I get it. Whatever happens is not because of you."

"Do you think I should have called him that day?"

Butler shrugged. "Probably. It wouldn't have changed what was happening. I still fucked up either way."

"But you wouldn't have hidden it."

"There's a problem going down at the club, and if I distracted him right now, he might not have seen it. It doesn't matter which way we look at this, Mandy. I was fucked one way or the other." He pushed some hair off her face, taking in her beauty once again. "You work all the time?"

"Yeah, pretty much. I like to keep busy. Why?"

"I was thinking about going away for a little while."

"Where?" she asked.

"I don't know. Dick went away for some time, and when he came back he seemed stronger for it. More put together. He's not had one of these mega crashes that I've had."

"You're thinking about going on a vacation?"

"Yeah. I've got some money put aside. If I arrange everything, you'll come?"

"Of course. I'll have to talk to some clients and make sure I can take a week."

"Make it a couple of weeks," he said.

"You're sure?"

"Yes. It's what we both need. You, me, some really bright sunshine. I think it'll work wonders."

"Excellent." She smiled, snuggling up against him.

Silence fell between them, but it wasn't uncomfortable. Butler just enjoyed the feel of having her in his arms, running the tips of his fingers up and down her back, feeling her breath against his neck. Peace settled over him, and it was so sudden that it shocked him. For the past couple of months, Mandy had plagued his thoughts. He'd wanted her, but he'd also felt that pull, the need for the drugs that had once controlled his entire life. They'd found a weakness within him, and he'd been unable to shake it, even though he was desperate to do it.

Kissing the top of her head, he teased her hair, pulling her head back to stare into her eyes.

"What are you thinking?" she asked.

"Nothing important right now." He pressed his lips to hers, and then he heard a loud growl.

Pulling back, he saw that Mandy's cheeks were on fire, and he started laughing. "We need to order some food," he said. "That's another bad of mine. I fuck you into oblivion, I must feed you."

He kissed her again, then moved away from the

bed. Grabbing his cell phone, he saw the number for the pizza place and put in a large order.

"We could have cooked," Mandy said, crawling to the edge of the bed. She wrapped her arms around his neck, pressing kisses to his skin.

He closed his eyes, enjoying the feel of her against him. "Yeah, well, I don't like the thought of waiting." He pulled her around so that she sat in his lap. Tilting her head back, he claimed her lips once again.

His cock started to stir, and she wrapped her fingers around his length.

Sliding his hands down her body, he cupped her pussy. Neither of them broke from the kiss, and he didn't want to either. Her lips consumed him, calmed him. He loved the feel of her on him, wrapped around him.

Her scent, her arms, everything calmed the beast within him, and that helped him to relax, to focus on her.

Dick's words came back to him.

The drugs still had the power they always had, but it was whether or not he was strong enough to ignore it, and he was.

This wasn't about Mandy, who he wanted more than anything else. This was about so much more than that.

This was about him, and being able to handle a drug-free and drama-free life, and he wanted that. He didn't just give up the drugs to be part of the club still, or because of Devil's need for them all to be clean. Butler gave them up because he wanted to. This wasn't a forced decision. He had to because he'd have been dead otherwise.

Now he just needed to prove to Mandy, to his club, to Devil, that the drugs didn't matter. He did.

****

"You did the right thing," Lexie said.

"That's not in question," Devil said, coming out of their bathroom while brushing his teeth. "I'm just so fucking pissed off."

"You always said this was a risk."

"But I didn't anticipate it now. I mean, come on, if anyone was going to crack wouldn't it have been when we were in the middle of all that shit, rather than at peace with everything? The most drama we've had is Simon nearly getting suspended from school."

"And like always, you took care of it." Lexie smiled over at her husband. "What do you think will happen?"

"Butler will take some time. He should have done it months ago, to be honest. Dick left, and found himself a woman."

"Butler's woman is right here though, Devil. You can't force him to go and find someone who is actually here."

Devil left and she heard him spit into the sink and clean it up, which again made her smile. Year of being married to each other and one of her pet peeves was the disgusting state of the sink as he never cleaned it. Not anymore.

Their marriage had to have some give and take in all things, and she'd done her fair share of giving and Devil of taking.

"I need Butler to be strong again. To know that he's not taking drugs for the club but for himself." Devil climbed into bed, pulling her against him, and she snuggled in his arms. Running her hands up and down his thick arms, she tilted her head back.

"Enough about Butler. He'll come good, I have no doubt about that."

"No doubt?"

"None whatsoever. His entire life is the club. We

SAM CRESCENT

all know it. So, there's something else coming up soon," she said.

"Something else?"

"Yes, something very important."

"There is?" Devil frowned. "I'm going to deal with Naked Fantasies being closed. It earns a lot for the club, but we'll be back in business within a month. Lola has already put out an advertisement looking for strippers."

She rolled her eyes. "This is so not about the club or the strippers. Come on, Devil, you know there is something." She paused waiting for him to figure it out. When he still hadn't said anything, she gasped. "Please tell me you remember?" she asked.

"Remember?"

"What is so important in a couple of weeks times?"

"That it's a couple of weeks?" he asked.

Lexie jerked back and there was still confusion in his eyes. "Seriously? You don't know."

"I know it's not your birthday or any of the kids'."

She shoved his chest and stormed out of the bed.

"Hey, where are you going?"

"How is it that out of everything you can remember, you can never, ever, remember when we first met?" She folded her arms, staring at him.

Devil was one of the hardest men she'd ever known, but when the club wasn't there, he was also the most romantic person in her life. Yes, he fucked up on occasion, but he always seemed to know exactly how to make it right. Staring at him, she waited.

"Our anniversary?"

"Not of when we got married either. It was the first day we met."

"Back at the strip club?"

"Yes," she said.

"This is always important to you. Every single year," he said.

"Meeting you changed my entire life, Devil. I don't even like to think where I'd be right now if it wasn't for our babies. They certainly wouldn't have been born."

He got off the bed and moved toward her. When he wrapped his arms around her waist, she didn't fight him. She never did. He always had that way about him that she never wanted to. "That one day changed the rest of my life as well, baby, but for me it's not just about that. It's about every single day. Waking up next to you, being inside you, loving you every second of every single day. That one day is not important."

"It is to me."

"I know, and believe me, after all this time, I'm going to make it up to you."

"You are?"

"Yes. I promise."

She smiled. "I can't wait."

"You're going to love it."

Chapter Nine

"This is fucking disgusting," Butler said, picking up a used condom. He now saw why the latex gloves were necessary. The club was gross, especially after a party, and he was finally seeing it through Mandy's eyes. He'd always found the latex gloves incredibly hot. He had this little doctor thing going on in his mind, but right now, that was completely replaced.

So horrible.

"You know you didn't have to come here. I did say."

All morning he'd assisted Mandy from one just to another. The lawyer's office was in fact the cleanest job they'd been on. Some light vacuuming and dusting and they were done. A couple of the houses where she worked were not great. Scum around the bath, and cigarette butts on the floor, but Mandy had done it. She'd kept on cleaning.

Then they had gotten to the clubhouse, and even though it had hurt to step inside the club without his leather cut, he'd needed to do this. Even though his club brothers had been shocked to see him without his cut and carrying some cleaning equipment, he'd done so with his head held high.

He was going to prove his spot, and make sure they knew he was not only clean physically, but also mentally.

"Think about something else," Mandy said, leaning on her mop.

"What?"

"Think about what cleaning this mess means. For a long time, it was all about finding that brand new place I always wanted or fixing my car for repairs."

"And now?"

"I got to see you."

This made him pause as he turned toward her. "Me?"

"Yes. You were always here, and I liked that. At first, I thought it was scary and that you were making sure I wasn't stealing anything, and now I know it's because you found me so intoxicating. You couldn't resist."

Even as she flirted with him, there was a red tinge to her cheeks that made her look incredibly cute.

"You're right, I couldn't resist." He moved so that he was bent over, his ass in the air. "You would drive me crazy when you were bent underneath stuff, wriggling your ass. It would make me think about fucking you, slapping your ass."

"Yeah, well now you don't have to think."

"No, I can plan it, but you see now I'm thinking about the other thing I want."

"And what is that?" she asked.

"Spreading the cheeks of your ass and taking that one hole of yours I've not claimed."

She rolled her eyes. "You will never get points for romance, Butler. Be aware of that."

"Do you want romance?" he asked.

Mandy shrugged. "It's not important."

"It is to me. I want to know what you want, and if romance is it, then I'm willing to give it a try," he said, sitting on the floor, and then wincing, thinking about what he'd been cleaning off the floor.

"I don't know what it is that I want. I guess I'd like to be able to rely on the man in my life. Not be afraid of him flying off the handles. I've never experienced romance, not once in my life, so I can't exactly crave something I've never had, can I?"

Her cell phone began to ring.

"Excuse me."

He watched her leave and knew that she was about to get more work. Cleaners were needed everywhere, and he'd only been with her a day. He was exhausted, and she had to be as well. He wondered if this helped her deal with her life, to get it back on track.

Butler finished up cleaning the space in the bathroom before heading outside to where he'd caught Devil with some of his kids.

Several of the club brothers slapped him on the back, and he smiled. Leaving the clubhouse, he stood back a bit, but so Devil saw that he was waiting.

"We're not on bad terms, Butler. You can approach. I'm not going to shoot you in front of my kids. Lexie tells me it's bad having it out in front of them. How have you been?" Devil's arms were folded as he turned slightly to him.

"I've been good. Better. I mean, the club is my life, but I understand clearly why you had to do what you had to do. I get it." He ran fingers through his hair, feeling that annoyance build. "I was wondering if it would be okay for me to take Mandy away for a couple of weeks. She's not had a break in a really long time, and I'd like to give this a try."

"You have any doubts this won't work between the two of you?"

"I know Dick took time away, and it put shit into perspective for him."

"Yeah, he even came home with an old lady to boot." Devil rubbed at his chin. "With all due respect, I'm into pussy, Butler. I'm the wrong person you should be asking."

Butler chuckled. "Mandy loves this job. She loves to work, and even though I think it's gross as shit, I think it calms her."

"Mandy's jobs … all of them, will be here when she gets back. I'll make sure of it." Devil looked at him. "She going to be your old lady?"

"That's what I'm hoping. I'm also wanting to get my old patch back."

"You're looking better," Devil said.

"It has been a couple of days."

"And already you're doing well. That is a very good sign, my friend." Devil nodded and turned back to look at his kids.

Everyone at the club knew how much Devil loved his family. He was the man everyone thought would never settle down, that a town, the life they'd seen The Skulls have, wasn't the way forward, and yet here they were, Devil being one of the most settled of all.

Heading back inside, Butler found Mandy back in the bathroom.

"Taking a lunch break already? You're slacking off, mister." She winked at him, and he pulled her into his arms.

"You can take it out of my pay."

"You think I'm paying you?"

He slammed his lips down on hers, silencing her. His cock instantly hardened but he'd have to wait to fuck her, which he was fine with. Being with Mandy was a dream come true in itself.

"We're going away tomorrow."

"We are?"

"Yes. You, me, a sandy beach, and lots of sex."

"What about work?"

"You don't have to worry about that. A couple of weeks alone together. You willing to take that chance with me?"

"I'm willing to take any chance." She wrapped her arms around his neck. "First, we really need to get this place cleaned."

"Let me grab a few more supplies from the car." He patted her ass, leaving her alone. On the way to the car, he saw Natalie sitting at the bench, notebook in hand, sketching something.

It had been a few days since he'd seen her. Stopping by her table, he dropped down. "Hey," he said.

"Butler, I've been wanting to see you. Slash told me what happened." She immediately closed her book. The look of concern touched him. "How are you?"

"I guess Slash told you everything."

"About you having drugs on you or in your room." She kept nodding her head.

"Yeah, I fucked up. That's what happened."

"You didn't take them though?"

"No, I didn't. Even though I didn't take them, it still doesn't matter, Natalie. I shouldn't have had them."

"This club means everything to you."

"I know, and I'm going to get my patch back."

"I see that you're with Mandy. Is that a good thing?" she asked. "You know, with your crush, I mean, how is that working?"

"Are you trying to gossip with me?"

"Do you love her?" Natalie asked.

Butler stared at her, not sure how to answer that. "I've got feelings for her."

"Good," Natalie said. "I ... I never wanted to make a choice between you and Slash."

"It wasn't a choice. We both knew that. You and I, we wouldn't have worked. You were scared, and I guess both of us gave you a good reason to ignore us."

"It gave me something." She sighed. "I'm so sorry about this whole thing."

"Don't be. You're a good friend." He patted her hand before he got up to leave. Natalie was an easy woman. She was nice, sweet, kind, but she didn't make him feel the way Mandy did, which was probably one of the reasons he initially went for her.

She didn't make it hard for him as he had nothing to win with her.

When it came to Mandy though, she was his prize.

****

A couple of days later

Mandy lifted her face up to the sun. The heat wasn't overpowering, but then she was wearing a light summer dress with thin straps. She couldn't recall ever having spent time at the beach, just relaxing. Her life hadn't allowed her to spend time away from work.

"You okay there?" Butler asked, moving up behind her.

He wrapped his arms around her waist, pressing a kiss to her neck.

"It's just so beautiful. I'm sorry. You must think this is incredibly lame of me."

"Far from it. I love looking at the beauty that surrounds us. This is not about judging here. You think this is beautiful, and I completely agree with you."

"You do?" She tilted her head back to look at the man that seemed to like messing with her head about everything.

"Yes, I do." He dropped a kiss to her lips. She loved it when he did that. In fact, she was finding lots of things she loved about him.

Butler was, in fact, the perfect gentleman with her. He opened doors for her, held her hand, rubbed her stomach during her period. Yes, they had gone on vacation, and she had hoped for them to really enjoy some good hard fucking, only for her period to start. Not that it mattered.

She loved his company, which was just another thing that she enjoyed about him. He could cook, and he also put the toilet seat down, which was a big deal for her. Oh, another thing, he put the lid on the toothpaste. Another bonus, and now she was starting to feel like a crazy person again.

Holding his arms where they lay, she settled back against him.

"How's your stomach?" he asked.

"Still cramping."

He moved his hand down and began to stroke her abdomen.

"I think this sucks the most."

He chuckled. "I'm a patient man here, Mandy. Besides, I like you reading to me, or us playing games, or enjoying a couple of movies."

"You don't want to fuck me?" she asked.

He growled against her ear and pressed his cock to her ass. "More than anything I want to do that, but I also know that's not going to happen. I like being with you though. Believe me, that's a new experience."

"Being with a woman?"

"No. Enjoying her company and you don't belong to anyone else."

She licked her suddenly dry lips. "Who *do* I belong to?"

His hands tightened around her waist, and she released a little gasp. Her tits tightened, and he flicked her ear with his tongue. "You know the answer to that, but just this once, I'll let you know. You belong to me, and you have since the first moment you entered the club. Don't even try to pretend you don't."

He released her stomach but took her hand as they made their way across the shoreline. She watched the ocean waves coming in and out. She felt calm watching them, relaxed.

"I think I could get used to this," she said.

"Not working?"

"No. Spending vacations with you."

"I've got a permanent position open, and I think you could be the perfect woman for the job."

She chuckled. "See, zero points for romance."

"You want me to do that kind of crap in your books. Get you flowers that would wilt. I might as well buy you a rosebush in a pot and tend it for you for life than buy you one silly flower or a whole bunch of them. I mean, come on, who thinks that's romantic?" he asked.

"A lot of women do."

Butler snorted. "And you see this is where the consumerist wins here."

"How does it?" Mandy asked.

She liked his little outbursts and his points of view. At times she found them so infuriatingly accurate, and other times completely stupid.

"All right, you want to know?"

"I said so, didn't I? Come on, wise guy, show me your point."

He stopped.

His hands were on her hips, and she loved the thrill that she always got when he touched her. She didn't know how he did it, but the moment he held her and looked at her, it was like she was the only woman in the world that mattered to him.

"Okay, flowers, roses, they're all supposed to be a sign of love? Of romance."

"That is correct."

"They all die."

"Excuse me?"

"You cut a flower from the bush, it has a limited amount of time to enjoy it, ergo, death. Every single relationship is doomed to fail for that method."

She wrinkled her nose. "I've seen Devil take Lexie lots of flowers. Their love grows from strength to strength."

"Very good point, but his garden is full of them."

"What?"

"Roses, flowers, he plants them for her to enjoy. Every now and then he'll go and cut a few stems to take to her, but his love has grown. That for me is what should happen. Flowers that are already pre-cut are doomed. It's why you'll never get a single flower or a bunch of them. You'll get bushes of them."

She couldn't help the smile that came to her face. "You know, for someone who is not romantic, that was pretty much there." She quickly looked away to deal with the tears in her eyes. Batting them away, she smiled at Butler. "Now that we've started, you've got to tell me your thoughts on other items."

"Are you getting me primed for Valentine's Day next year?"

"No, I'm not. I'm curious. That's the first time I've ever heard someone view flowers like that."

"I totally rocked your world with it though."

"Yes, so your thoughts on chocolates?" she asked.

"Overrated. Let's face it, if anyone finishes a whole box, they're going to barf. Also, what does a woman buy herself to get over a messy breakup?" he asked.

"Chocolates or cake."

"Exactly. It's like the guy is instantly turning around and saying, 'Hey, I'm going to break your heart, but here is the makeup chocolate you don't even have to pay for.'"

"Wow, I find that fascinating. Okay, what about

jewelry?" she asked.

"There's only one piece of jewelry that anyone is interested in, and that's the engagement ring. Everything else is always set to disappoint."

"Not everything. Earrings could be nice."

"But in a relationship they're not going to cut it. I don't know; jewelry is a sticky subject for me. I think unless you're all in, you shouldn't buy the stuff."

They stopped at an ice cream stand.

"Want one?" he asked.

They waited for their order. Butler didn't let go of her hand as he pulled out some cash to pay for their ice cream. Once they had theirs, they continued back toward their beach house. It was a beautiful place.

The first day they arrived, she gave it a thorough clean, which took a couple of hours as there was a lot of dust. Not that she minded. Once the house was clean, they checked the food and went shopping.

She loved the domestic feeling she got with Butler. No other man had ever helped her to feel so laid back, nor had she ever wanted to be part of it.

"I've told you my reasons, so now what do you find romantic?" he asked.

"I did find flowers and chocolates romantic, but that has been completely blown apart, and I'm never looking at them the same way again. I mean, seriously, that sucked big time." She licked at her chocolate ice cream. "I don't really know. I've never really gotten flowers or jewelry from anyone. Chocolate is always good, no matter the occasion. I hate those coffee chocolate things that everyone seems to put in though. I find them gross, and the toffees. I always think they're going to ruin my teeth."

He chuckled. "We're talking about romance here, and you've turned it toward a dental appointment."

She laughed with him, resting her head against his shoulder. "I don't know. I guess spending time with the person. Getting to know them without fear of hurting one another. We both have a past, and it doesn't hurt either of us to learn about that. Then of course I find meals romantic."

"Meals?"

"You know, dinner by candlelight. Dressing up in beautiful clothes, the stars above, good food, maybe some wine or some really good sparkling water in our case. Conversation, and just a lovely meal where you're not scared about what will come next. Yes, I think that's romantic. Are you going to put a little downer on it? Maybe say steaks have been slaughtered, or the chicken was mistreated and how that will ruin the mood?"

"No, I think a good meal is the best romantic gesture of all."

They were outside their beach house, which overlooked the stunning view of the ocean. They sat down on one of the boulders that was there. She rested her head on his arm.

"Do you miss it?" she asked.

"The club?"

"Yes."

"Yeah, I miss it."

"How have your thoughts been about … you know?" She bit her lip, not wanting to bring up bad memories.

"How have my thoughts been about the drugs?"

She winced.

"You don't have to worry, sweetheart. If I can't say it like it is, then I'm doing something wrong, aren't I? I've not thought about them, not in the way of taking them. I've thought about them and what I almost did. It makes me angry that I nearly threw away my life for a second time because of it."

"You didn't though."

"It doesn't make it exactly hurt any less, does it?" He sighed. "I want to get my patch back at the club so bad, but there's something I want to ask you first."

"Go ahead."

"When I get my patch back, I want you to be my old lady."

She stared up at him, a little shocked. "You do?" She knew what an old lady meant to these men. He was asking her to belong to him, and even though they teased about it now, this was the commitment that Devil was talking about.

Mandy expected the churning in her stomach or the fear, or something else, something more dangerous, but it didn't come. In fact, she felt ... excited. Exhilarated that that he wanted her to be his in every single way that counted.

"You're being serious right now?"

"Deadly serious."

"Oh, my, I ... yes, I would be yours, Butler."

She dropped the remains of her melting ice cream onto the ground and held him close.

Feeling his arms wrapped around him was the best and most romantic feeling in the world to her.

Chapter Ten

"Do you want to tell me why you want to learn to make oatmeal chocolate chip cookies?" Lexie asked, placing the last of the ingredients on the table. Simon stood, looking his rebellious self but also a little nervous.

"Tabby likes them, and I like her."

Lexie smiled.

He was growing up way too fast for her. She ruffled his head, and he growled. Out of the corner of her eye, she watched him smooth his hair back into place, quickly checking the mirror to make sure it was okay.

"Are you still writing to her?" Lexie asked.

"Yes." He pulled from his jeans pocket the letter she knew he'd gotten an hour ago in the mail. "Here it is."

"You want to read it out to me?"

He rolled his eyes.

"I can if you really want to hear it."

"Of course I do, silly. Come on, stop being a party pooper."

Simon opened up the neatly folded letter, and she knew without a doubt that they would go with the others he had in a shoebox in his drawer beside his bed. He read them all constantly. Whenever he was angry or feeling alone, she would find him reading them.

His connection to Tabby was helping to draw him out.

"'Dear Simon.'" He stopped and looked up at her. "She always starts that way. She says it's the best way of starting a letter. Dear sir, madam, that kind of thing."

"I get it. Go on."

"'I really enjoyed the summer with you this year, and Mom's already working on you guys coming over next. She thinks it will be a great break for Lexie. She says that with all the kids your mom works so hard, and she's right. You have a lot of brothers and sisters, Simon.'" He looked up again. "She put a smiley face next to it. 'I'm not looking forward to going back to school though. Before school let out for the summer, the school merged with another in the town over, and they are horrible. There's a couple of boys in the classroom, and I know Dad wants them to be gone soon. He doesn't like us all mingling together. I don't like them, and a couple of them are from a rival MC, which does upset Dad. Nothing we can do about it though. Both schools were failing, and this was in the works for a long time. I'm sorry if I'm venting too much. I can't wait until we can chat online. It'll be so much easier, but … I don't like it. Daisy gets bullied, and Anthony has been in so many fights and so has Miles.'"

Lexie knew all about the merger of the two schools, as Eva had talked about it. The town over had another MC, which had never bothered The Skulls. They had settled down a couple of years ago, had a sit-down with Lash, and things had been moving on just fine from then. Now their kids were mingling, and with it came their own problems.

"'What are you doing for Halloween? I don't care that it's early, but I want to dress up as a princess this year like I do every single year, only I'm going to scare it up. I've been learning some new tricks so expect pictures, and I hope it's gruesome for you. I can't stay long. I really need to go. I'm spending the day with Darcy, but she is a little boring right now. She has a mega crush on Ink, but you cannot say anything, not a word, okay. Promise me. I can't wait for your next letter. They are the best kind of letters in the world. Love you like always, Tabby. P.S. sorry about the crumbs and grease marks. I'm eating oatmeal chocolate chip cookies, and they are my favorite.'" He finished and looked up. "Do you think we can move closer?"

"That's not going to happen. So that's why you're wanting to learn to make the cookies. They're Tabby's favorite."

He didn't say anything, but she saw he was struggling with something. "Mom, do you think how I feel about Tabby is stupid?"

"No, I don't. Why?"

"Some of the boys at school, they think it's stupid."

"Boys can be stupid."

"Dad's not happy."

"Only because he doesn't like what that means to him."

"What does it mean?"

"She's a Skull, Simon. That can bring complications. There could be a merger there, or you could decide to cut off and take a Skull patch, or quit the club altogether."

"I'm going to be part of Chaos Bleeds," Simon said. "I want that. I want to be in my dad's club."

"When we get older our decisions change. I never thought I'd be married to your father, have so many kids, and help run a fashion shop. I didn't even know if I'd make it past thirty years old. Life takes us in so many different directions. It's not a bad thing though."

"It's not?"

"No. How do you feel about Tabby?" she asked.

"When I'm with her, she's the only girl in the world for me. She makes me happy and I can't think of anything else or feel. I can't stand the thought of her being hurt or upset. I love her. I want to take care of her."

"Those kinds of feelings are not stupid, Simon. Don't ever let anyone tell you any differently. You're young, but that doesn't make you any different from the rest of us. Now, go and wash your hands so I can teach you how to make these cookies."

****

"Morning, beautiful," Butler said, watching as Mandy stretched her arms above her head. Her tits thrust out, and it took every part of him not to reach out and cup her.

"You've been watching me sleep again?"

"I can't help it. You're a beautiful woman to watch sleep."

"You've got all the nice words to say. I must look a sight."

"You don't wear makeup, so it's not smudged. Besides a little drool," he pointed to the corner of her mouth, "you look very sexy."

"Ew." She quickly covered her mouth and climbed out of the bed. She wore a pair of shorts and a thin top. He watched her walk into the bathroom.

Climbing from the bed, he followed her, watching as she quickly brushed her teeth.

"I was only kidding."

"Yeah, well, it wasn't funny." She finished brushing her teeth and turned toward him. "I have bed hair."

"It's pretty hair," he said, pulling her in close. Kissing her lips, he sank his fingers into the length, holding her in place.

"What are the plans for today?" she asked.

"We can go and do some exploring, if you'd like." When he first negotiated this trip, he had hoped to spend every single day screwing her. They had the perfect excuse to get away, but so far, they hadn't even been able to enjoy that. She'd been on her period a couple of days now, and the cramps had stopped.

"I'd like that."

"Excellent. I'll let you get dressed and I'll get started on breakfast." He went to walk away, but she stopped him, wrapping her arms around his waist, and holding him close. Butler closed his eyes, loving her arms holding him a little too much. "What was that for?" he asked, when she stepped back.

He wasn't about to mourn the loss of her touch, not yet.

"I just love spending time with you. Being here, it really … thank you."

He got the sense that she wanted to say a whole lot more but held back.

Leaving her to get dressed, he quickly got their breakfast underway.

Before they had left Piston County, he'd gotten Lexie to organize several dresses for Mandy as he knew she didn't possess a single one, which was fine. It was turning into one of the hottest summers on record, and he wanted her to be comfortable. Jeans and a shirt were not going to cut it. For him, they could have stayed home all day, butt ass naked, but that didn't happen.

Mandy joined him and started cleaning around him as he cooked. They had developed a routine, which he found incredibly comfortable. The more time he spent with her, the more he realized how much he loved her little quirks, like her need to have her hair tied up in a band first thing in the morning, but by the middle of the day, it was falling all over the place. Her need to clean constantly, he loved. She had a cloth in her hand, wiping things down, and she also organized the books. The owner of the villa that he'd rented from would arrive to find their small library neatly organized. She'd done the same with the DVD collection. Again, cute.

He loved taking care of her though, opening

doors, holding her hand. They were little things that he'd once taken for granted, or even mocked with other guys. He knew some of the club members were not interested in settling down, and that was fine. For a long time now, he'd been watching the guys that had, and he'd felt that overwhelming need to have a family. He wanted a woman he loved to go home to. Who put a smile on his face the way he'd seen Lexie do for Devil, or Judi for Ripper. He could go on and on. Even Martha put a smile on Dick's face, and that was saying something.

That man was the biggest asshole on the planet, no doubt about that.

For a long time, Butler didn't think he'd ever want kids or a family, or a life like that, only now he did.

Mandy put their knives and forks on the table, and he finished up his food. He could have a family with her, and he knew without a doubt that he'd be happy. She put that smile on his face and made him look forward to waking up.

He loved her.

That's what he'd been fighting for so long.

Even before they had sex, and he only got to see her cleaning, he'd fallen for her. She wasn't like any other woman he'd been with. Yes, their pasts were messed up, but that wasn't who they were right now. They were different.

"You okay?" Mandy asked, moving up beside him. "You've gone a little pale." She placed a hand on his back.

"Yeah, yeah, I'm fine. Just hungry."

He served them both up a plate and was aware of Mandy's concerned gaze. They talked about what was in the newspaper, nothing of any real importance. He was still reeling from his own sudden clarity.

Mandy was the woman he loved.

She was the one who made his heart race, and his hands clammy.

"Okay, you're starting to worry me. Are you okay?" Mandy asked.

He stared down at where her hand held his and nodded. "Yeah, of course I am. I'm perfectly fine." He kissed her knuckles.

"You'd tell me if something was wrong?"

"Yes, you know I would."

They finished their breakfast. Mandy kept looking at him, and he liked her worry. It meant she had feelings for him too.

After they finished breakfast, she cleaned up their dishes and the kitchen while he quickly pulled on some clothes. Grabbing his cell phone, he dialed the only person he knew he could speak to.

"Hello," Natalie said, giving out a little moan that told him he'd woken her up.

"Who the fuck is that?" Slash asked.

"It's me," Butler said."

"It's Butler."

"What the fuck does he want?"

"Shut up. What's wrong, Butler? Everything okay with Mandy?"

"Yeah, everything is fine." He glanced at the door to see no sign of Mandy. "I … erm … could you put Slash on the phone? It might be easier to talk to him."

"Sure. He wants to talk to you."

"What the fuck is all this about?" Slash asked. "You never call this early."

"How did you know?" Butler asked.

"How did I know what?"

"Your feelings for Natalie?" He checked again. Mandy was humming in the kitchen.

"Is this some kind of joke?"

"No joke. I just want to know the answers." He was trying not to freak out right now. He heard movement over the phone line.

"She's the only woman in the world that I care about. The other old ladies, I like them and I care for them. I'd die for them, but with Natalie, she's my entire world. I want to be everything for her, give her everything, be it all."

He could imagine them looking at each other right now, sharing that smile that he'd seen couples do.

"What is all this about?"

"I'm in love with Mandy."

"You're only just figuring that shit out now?" Slash asked. "We all knew."

"You all knew?" Butler frowned.

"You've been out of rehab a long time. You took all the jobs that no one wanted, and you had the club's back. Then Mandy started working at the club, and before long, you had a reason to be at the club all the time. You even followed her around, watching as she worked. It was kind of creepy, but your gaze would follow her. The old ladies were having bets on how long it would take you to realize it."

"Wait? What?"

"You heard me." Slash chuckled. "I can't wait to tell the boys. Have you told her yet?"

"I've only just realized it myself. I'm not about to tell her."

"Well, you better get on that. I'll let the guys know."

Before he could even say anything, he hung up, and Butler cursed.

"Is everything okay?" Mandy asked, standing in the doorway.

"Perfect. Really fucking perfect."

****

Butler was more distracted than usual, and Mandy tried not to panic on what that meant. After their talks, and the time they shared, she was really finding it hard to keep her feelings in check around him.

She found it natural now to reach out and touch his cheek, or run her fingers through her hair, and telling him how she really felt was on the tip of her tongue so many times. This vacation they were taking had helped her finally come face to face with her feelings for Butler.

When she got called away for her mother's murder she'd been struggling with her feelings for him, but she had kept it all in check. She was there to do a job, and Mia had helped her to get it. While she'd been in protective custody so they could track her stepfather, Butler had been the only guy she had thought about.

She had put it down to crazy fantasies, but being with him, knowing him, she knew it was a whole lot more than that.

For the first time in her entire life she had fallen in love, and it scared her. She'd never been with a guy long enough or wanted anyone enough to risk it.

They made their way around the market, and she stared at all the wonderful artisanal things on offer. She wasn't really paying attention as her thoughts were on the man beside her. Butler held her hand as they walked, and he wouldn't allow anyone to bump into them so they stood really close.

It was really hot, and she had finally finished her cycle that morning. He'd been a little distant of late, and she didn't want to ruin this feeling they had between them.

"Are you hungry?" he asked.

"Starving."

She stopped in a small restaurant that served

Italian food. She loved it just because it had air conditioning. Putting her bag on the floor between her feet, she smiled across at him, but he was looking past her shoulder.

Her nerves were frayed.

"Are you wanting to head back home?" she asked, wincing at her familiar use of the term "home."

"What?" he asked, his gaze returning to her.

"You seem kind of out of it. You've been like that all morning. Are you ready to go back to Piston County?" She pressed her lips together, more nervous than she'd ever been in her life.

"We've got another week yet. Of course not."

"Oh. Are you sure? I don't mind if you want to go back."

He reached out, taking her hands. "Do *you* want to go back?"

"No. I've really enjoyed my week away. I think it has been really kind of awesome actually." She stared down at their joined hands.

I love you, Butler, and right now I'm freaking out, and I don't know what to do.

"I'm loving being with you."

Her heart leapt at his words.

They pulled away as the waiter brought them over their food. Of course, they'd be the ones interrupted by the waiter.

Once they were served, the moment was lost, not that she'd have been able to say anything. The last thing she wanted to do was to spill her guts here in case he was feeling completely the opposite. People changed their minds all the time. She knew all about that.

This had never mattered to her. Falling in love wasn't something she'd thought would be a problem for her.

"So I wanted to talk to you about something," Butler said.

"Okay." She took a sip of her water. Everything felt lodged in her throat, but still, she waited.

"I was wondering what your thoughts are on family? I know we said that we'd never have kids or settle down. Would anything change your mind?"

She took a bite of the pasta, not really tasting the meaty sauce. "Erm, wow, this is a little out of the blue."

"I just … I'm curious. We all can change our minds."

She nodded. Family was something she had always wanted. After all the problems she had growing up with her mother, it had been like a mockery to her to even consider having a family.

"I … when I was a little girl … I always thought what it would be like to have the kind of family you see in the movies. You know the mother that cared, packed a school lunch. A dad that went out to work or something. I did want a family. I know I said that kids were not for me, but if I really think about it, and the fact I'm getting older, being thirty and all that, yes, I guess one day I hope to have a family. It's just … I've never been lucky enough for that option to be open to me." She pushed some hair out of her face and smiled. "Wow, I sound so morbid."

"Far from it."

"What about your stance?" she asked. "You didn't want kids, but you were so good that day."

"I drew the short straw."

"You had everything under control though. Do you want kids?"

"Do you promise not to run out screaming right now?" he asked.

"Yes."

"I want a boy and a girl." He stared past her shoulder once again. "Christmas morning I'd love to hear them both scream with excitement wondering if Santa had been there, and of course he had. The big guy will always come." He suddenly stopped. "I don't want to confuse you."

"No, it's just that you said you didn't want to have kids, and it sounds like you've thought a lot about it."

"If you don't want kids then that's cool. We'll figure something out."

She tilted her head to the side and smiled. "Would you like to have a family with me?"

This seemed like a big step, a huge one. Biting her lip, she waited for him to respond. He opened his mouth, but all of a sudden music began playing, and they looked toward the source to see an elderly couple surrounded by family.

She watched as the staff sang while also bringing out cake. Butler took her hand, and she looked down at them. Could it be possible to have a family surround them, singing and dancing for an anniversary?

It all seemed a little much. After the singing ended and the family left the restaurant, their food was finished. Butler paid, and they made their way back to their beach house. She didn't know what to say to fill the silence.

There were a lot of things left unsaid, but it also came with their own problems as well.

Were they moving too fast?

Could they make it together?

Outside of the beach house, she stopped, putting a hand on his chest.

"What's wrong?" he asked.

"I need to say something to you."

"Okay. It can't wait until we go inside?"

"Not right now. I need to get it out. When we go inside, you'll get naked, and we'll do a lot of other things, you know. I need to have a clear head."

He ran his hands up and down her arms, and she took a deep breath. His touch made it even harder for her to focus, so she caught his hands in hers, stopping him.

"For a long time, I've thought that I was unlovable. How can anyone ever love me? I was pushed to one side and forgotten. Then I went crazy, and I guess being used and doing a lot of using helped a lot. Family is something I've always wanted, but I've always found that it's a place that hurts the most. My mom hated me, and she died at the hands of yet another stepfather. The dream of having a family kind of left. When I'm with you though, I can feel and hope for things that I thought were no longer allowed for me to have." She glanced down at their hands. "I would like to take that chance with you, Butler. If you want to try to make this work. I don't know what we're going to be or how we're going to end up, but with you, I'd really love that chance more than anything else in the world."

Butler released her hands, and cupped her face, tilting her head back. "You want me to clear some things up?"

"What do you mean?"

"You're my woman, Mandy. I'm not going to throw you away or get bored. You're mine, and that means I'll be the man that you wake up to every single morning, and go to sleep with. I want to hold you in my arms as I fall, and never let go. The only thing in my life that I've craved is drugs, but then I saw you. From that moment on, nothing else in my crazy world has mattered to me. Grabbing those drugs, I think it was a way of trying not to take you. I want you to be here because you have a choice. The truth is … I love you."

Her mouth fell open.

Words failed her.

"There, I finally said it. I love you, and I want you to be my woman for the rest of our lives."

Well, he could be romantic, but of course it was mixed with his usual Butler charm.

Chapter Eleven

Saying it once was like getting over that jump that seemed to take everything out of you. Butler stared into her green eyes, ran his thumb across her lip, and said it again.

"I love you."

Mandy smiled, and he felt like screaming it from the top of his lungs. Instead, he pulled her close, and claimed her lips hard. Her hands slid up his chest, wrapping around the back of his neck.

He held her tightly to him, not wanting to let her go.

Gripping her ass, he lifted her up and moved her toward the door.

He tried to open the door, but of course they had locked it.

Growling in frustration, he put her down, and found the key. His hand shook a little, and Mandy took the key from him, opening the door.

Kicking it closed, he placed the key in the small dish and carried her through the house.

"Do you want to stop? Have a coffee?"

"For the past week I've been rubbing your stomach and dealing with your cramps. Tonight, I am going to be balls deep inside you and make up for lost time. Also, you're no longer allowed to wear clothes. I forbid it."

She giggled as he kicked the bedroom door only for it to remain closed. Mandy reached out, flicking it open.

"I am being thwarted in my mission."

"You're so cute," she said.

"Especially when I want something."

He finally put her on the feet. Turning her around,

he slid the catch of the zipper down her body.

He flicked the bra open and spun her back around.

Mandy swatted his hands away and began yanking on his shirt, pulling it up over his head. They fought each other to get naked first, and when they were, he pulled her close, her tits pressing against his chest.

Lifting her up, he placed her on the bed. Spreading her thighs open wide, he stared down at her creamy cunt. She was already so slick.

"You want me, baby?"

"Yes, I want you."

Stroking over her pussy, he pressed a finger to her core, watching as she took it. Adding a second finger, he relished her gasp, twisting around to stroke over her G-spot. Pulling his fingers from her pussy, he sucked them in his mouth, tasting her.

"I always knew you'd be so good."

Kneeling on the floor between her spread thighs, he spread the lips of her pussy, and licked his tongue between her slit. Circling her clit, he moved down to plunge inside her.

He took her hands, placing them on the lips of her pussy.

"I want you to keep yourself open for me. That's it, baby. Yeah, like that."

He pressed his fingers back into her pussy, plunging them in and out as he sucked on her clit. He kept changing the pace, going from rapid movements of his tongue, to slowing it down and making her burn with it.

Working that spot inside her, he waited until she was at the edge before removing his fingers. They were soaked in her cum, so he trailed them back, teasing over the puckered hole of her anus.

At first, she tensed, but as he kept up his strokes, she finally relented, and gave him what he wanted, which as far as he was concerned was such a pretty fucking sight.

Pushing the tip of one finger into her ass, he continued to lap at her clit. She shook with the pleasure. His name was constantly falling from her lips as he tormented her over and over again, but he didn't stop. There was no way for him to. His cock hurt he wanted inside her so badly.

Once he worked past that tight ring of muscles, he thrust his finger to the hilt, listening to her cries.

"Fuck!" she screamed, arching up.

In and out, he thrust his finger, waiting for her to get used to the feel of him before adding a second one.

All the time he kept up the teasing of her pussy, waiting for just the right moment to push her over the edge. After she'd taken two of his fingers and was riding them, sliding up and down on him, he finally let her go over that peak of her orgasm. Her ass tightened on him, squeezing him.

Only when she came down from her peak did he pull away. Leaving her spread-eagled on the bed, he quickly washed his hands before coming back to the bed.

Her arms were spread out, and she smiled at him.

"I never said this to you either, but I love you too. I do find it kind of scary. I've never been like this with anyone else before."

"It is scary. The scariest thing I've ever done."

"I want to be your woman, Butler. I'll be your old lady."

"You don't have a problem with me taking the patch again?" He stepped closer, cupping her face. His cock stood hard and proud, but he ignored it. Right now, the only woman that mattered was her, and he wanted to make this right for the both of them.

"No, why would you think I'd mind? The patch is part of who you are."

"Some women struggle with the life."

"I know you won't hurt me, Butler."

"My past?"

"Let's not do this, okay? We can both screw this up. You go on the drugs, and I sleep with everything. It's not going to happen, and I think I finally understand when people say you've got to learn to take risks like this. I'd rather risk being with you right now than never knowing what it would be like." She cupped his face, stroking his cheek. "We don't have a normal start, I get that. We're a little damaged, but together we could make this work, Butler. I'd like to try."

Pressing her back to the bed, he claimed her lips hard, sliding his tongue into her mouth, and she moaned. Her hand wrapped around his cock, working from the base up to the tip then down again.

Mandy pulled away from the kiss, and before he could stop her, her lips were around the head of his cock.

Wrapping her hair around his fist, he worked her mouth over his dick, forcing her to take him to the back of her throat, and he watched as she gagged. He did this a couple of times before she finally relaxed and swallowed him down.

Coming in her mouth wasn't what he wanted, so he pulled out before he lost complete control. The length was now covered in her saliva. Moving her to her knees toward the edge of the bed, he put the tip of his dick at her entrance.

Slowly, he began to fill her, making her take more of him as he cupped her hips and slammed to the hilt. They both cried out, and he felt the answering clench of her cunt around him.

Spreading her cheeks wide, he watched his cock as he began to pull out. When only the tip was inside her, he suddenly filled her, slapping her ass as he hit her cervix. She wriggled on his length, and he closed his eyes, counting to ten to gain some control.

He struggled to hold onto his sanity.

Over and over he pounded her pussy, and even though he wanted her ass right then, he knew he wasn't going to be satisfied until he'd filled her with his cum.

He slammed inside her, feeling her pussy clutch at him, holding him in like a vise. He didn't stop though, wanting her to scream his name.

Stroking her clit, he brought her to another orgasm before he finally found his release. Holding her hips so tight that he knew they would bruise, he released his cum deep in her cunt, knowing one day he'd do this and they'd make a baby.

****

Mandy giggled as he rolled her over and drew her knees back up beneath her.

"Are you ready?" she asked.

"Yes, and it only took thirty minutes."

Butler hadn't wanted to leave the bedroom so rather than fight, he'd demanded they play a game of "eye spy," which was a really weird thing to do, but he would come up with silly names for things, which she didn't get. All the while, he timed how long it would take for him to get a hard-on.

"You do know that I'm taking this to the grave with me," Mandy said. "This is not romantic or sexy."

"We'll do things a little differently in our house."

"Timing how long it takes you to get an erection after just coming, that is a little different, I grant you that." She closed her eyes and gasped as he teased her clit, his fingers stroking over her button before sliding down to plunge inside her.

She couldn't think when he did that.

"Well, considering my game is supposed to be a little childish, you're very aroused there, baby. So wet and ready for me."

"I'm only human."

"I know, and I love it. My only *human* woman." He drew his fingers back, and she closed her eyes.

He teased across her anus, going in circles and pressing against her ass. When he did that pleasure erupted around her body, and she pushed out as the tip of his finger slid inside her.

The thought of him owning every single part of her body thrilled her. She wanted him to have her, to possess her, to take her. Her body belonged to him just as her heart did as well.

He worked her with one finger, then added a second.

Only when he was ready did he place the tip of his cock against her ass.

Biting her lip, she waited, as the head was much bigger than his two fingers. Closing her eyes, she held her breath and pushed out as he started to work his cock in.

Inch by inch, she waited as he filled her, thrusting his dick inside her. When he was all the way in, he tapped her ass.

"You're so fucking tight." He ran his fingers up and down her back, stroking her.

There was pain but also pleasure.

She felt weird, like she wanted to push him out but didn't want to let him go either. Reaching between her thighs, she stroked her pussy, teasing the hard bud, sliding her fingers down to fill her pussy, drawing more of their combined cum over her clit.

Butler began rocking inside her, slow strokes to start with, letting her get accustomed to the sheer size of his cock.

When he was all the way out, he plunged back inside, and she cried out. Again, the pain and pleasure mingling were almost too much and not enough at all.

Sinking her teeth into her lip, she played with her pussy, and Butler took her ass. He kept spreading her ass apart, and she imagined him watching them, seeing his cock slide into her ass.

Just the thought of it turned her on even more.

"You like being my kind of dirty little bitch?" he asked.

"Yes."

"Good, because I like you like that. I want that when we're alone together. I want you to get as bad and dirty as you can be. Don't hide what you want. I will use your body, Mandy. I will fuck you and give you more pleasure than you can ever imagine, but I will take as well. I want you to take from me, to use me how you want to."

He pounded inside her three thrusts, and this time there wasn't as much pain. In fact, there wasn't any pain at all, and she gasped at the sudden heat of pleasure.

"You like that, Mandy? You like me fucking your ass, making it mine?" He filled her again, fucking her. His grip tightened on her hips as he took over.

She kept on playing with her clit, feeling that peak starting to build. She pressed back against his thrusts, wanting him deep inside her ass, to feel him pulse as he filled her.

Her own orgasm took her by surprise as she screamed his name.

His cock seemed to get bigger as she came, her ass squeezing him with each wave of her orgasm.

Butler slapped her ass, slammed inside her, and growled her name as his cock pulsed, spurting his hot cum deep inside her.

She closed her eyes as he collapsed over her. His cock was still within her, but there was no chance of her moving. Right now, he'd taken over every part of her mind and body.

"I'll move in a second," he said.

"Why? We can stay passed out here for another couple of days."

"I'm not wasting a couple of days. I'm going to want to fuck you again."

She giggled. "I love that you can't get enough of me." She pushed some of her hair off her face.

Butler wrapped his arms around her, kissing her neck and shoulder. She closed her eyes once again, feeling an overwhelming love for this man.

Neither of them spoke, and as the exhaustion eased, it came with some peace.

"I'm going to go and run us both a bath."

"Okay." He pulled out of her ass, and she moaned as he spread her ass wide again.

"What are you doing?" she asked, giggling.

"I'm watching my cum leak out of you."

"You're a dirty bastard."

"Yeah, and you love it, so stop your whining." He slapped her ass, and she yelped as he sank his teeth into the flesh. Watching him leave the room, she pulled the pillow beneath her head and laughed.

She couldn't recall a time when she had been this happy, this contented.

Seconds later, Butler returned, and he helped her up, carrying her through to the bathroom, where he placed her in the tub. He followed her, though, climbing in behind her so that she rested back against him.

He took hold of her hands and locked their fingers together.

"What do you think your club will say?" Mandy asked.

"They're going to love it. The girls love a reason to celebrate, and our getting together will be a big fucking reason." He kissed her neck.

Wrapping his arms around her, she stared ahead. "How will you get your patch back?"

"By proving that I know what I want. That the drugs are a problem, but I can handle it."

She tilted her head back. "I'll do whatever I can to help."

"Good, if I ever start using at all, I want you to go straight to Devil."

"Why do I not like the sound of that?"

"I wasn't always a good person, Mandy. I want you to promise me you'd do that."

"You're not going to use again. I know you're not."

"Promise me."

"I promise, Butler."

"I love you, Mandy, and to me you're worth fighting for."

She stared at him for the longest time and knew he'd have something in place. Devil would take care of it. She wouldn't ever let that happen.

When it came to Butler, she was in this for life, and there was no getting out of it, not for her.

****

"What are you doing in here late at night?" Lexie asked, stepping into Devil's office.

"I am accepting an invitation to a very interesting picnic slash barbeque, slash potential bloodbath."

"Is this that thing I've heard you and Lash talking

about? I thought this already happened and you turned it down," Lexie said, picking up the fancy envelope.

"It was, and then for some reason or another, it got canceled, and then new invitations were sent out. I just got off the phone with Lash, and he's going to accept."

"The Billionaire Bikers MC, sounds like a rock band."

Devil blew out a breath. "They're … not a real MC. At least, I don't consider them to be. Not in the sense of the club. They're all fucking rich as shit, silver spoon kind of crap."

"You're blasting them, but I sense a little respect there, honey. What's going on?" Lexie said.

Devil pulled her down into his lap. He held her hip and leaned back, aware of her gaze on him. "They do good deeds."

"And that's a bad thing?"

"No, it's actually a really good thing when I think about it. They deal mostly in trafficking."

"How can that be a good thing? It's illegal."

"No, no, not what I meant. They're the ones that have broken a couple of trafficking rings and provided sanctuary for women that have been rescued. Some of the women they have been able to save before anything really bad has happened to them, but there have been others that were not so lucky." He took the fancy card out of her hands. "They've invited the clubs, as you know, to a fancy picnic. Don't know what it's for yet."

"You think they're reaching out?"

"Could be a reach out. Only way of finding out is to check it out, right?"

"When is it for?"

"End of the summer."

"Cool," Lexie said. "I'll be sure to wear my fancy

dress."

"Whatever you wear will be fancy."

"You know how to say all the right things."

"Butler and Mandy are arriving back tomorrow," he said.

"Oh, is this a good or bad thing?" she asked.

"I'm hoping it was a good thing."

"How was the drug thing?"

"I dealt with Michael, and he took the stripper and the pimp." He ran a hand down his face.

"How are you dealing with it all though?" she asked.

"What do you mean?"

"For so long you've been the guy to make all the decisions."

"I know."

"Now you're calling up Michael and the Feds, and getting them to resolve matters. I know you put on a brave face for it all, but this is me, Devil. Speak honestly."

He didn't like how she seemed to know everything he was thinking.

Stroking her cheek, he stared into her eyes.

Most of his life before coming to Piston County he didn't believe in love. He didn't even think that he was capable of such a strong emotion. Meeting Lexie had completely blown his entire world apart. Piece by piece, he realized he was only living part of a life. The moments he craved more than anything were these.

"It's hard, baby. I'm not going to lie. It … it would be a lot easier to just kill them. I've got a nice big clubhouse for me to bury their bodies. But—and this is the pretty big but—a huge one."

"What is it?"

"I've got you and my babies, Lex. Killing these

people is easy. Where one falls, another rises, and that is all that happens. One down, two up, three up, and it goes on and on. There has to come a point when I realize dealing with the club, taking care of my family is where my focus should be."

"You're not going to regret this, are you?"

"No. I'm not. The decision to stop the drugs and the gun runs wasn't an easy one. I didn't just flick a switch and think, 'We're the good guys now.' I thought long and hard. I thought about you, our kids, Kayla." He saw the pain in her eyes.

"Why Kayla?"

"Because her death hurt you in a really bad way. Ashley's death. That young woman, club whore or not, didn't deserve to die. The men we've lost, the pain they've suffered. We've done enough," Devil said. "Too much. We've loved, we've lost, and it has been a fucking heartbreak of a journey, which was why I decided to do this. To call Michael, to go legit, to help others. I'll never regret that."

She cupped his face, and he held her tightly.

While he had his wife, Devil knew he would fight to the ends of the earth to keep all the bad shit at bay.

Chapter Twelve

One week later

Back in Piston County, Butler didn't go to Devil to tell him that he'd found his place and that he'd also taken his woman. Instead, he made a home with Mandy. He helped her get back into the swing of things with her cleaning work. He saw his club brothers around town and there was a wish that he could wear his leather cut, but at the same time, he wanted to earn it.

The old ladies had started to accept Mandy into their circle, and they had taken her under their wing. Not only did she clean now, but she'd been pulled into the schedule of taking care of the shop, babysitting, and even being there at the club get-togethers, which was why they were pulling into the Chaos Bleeds clubhouse.

He turned the ignition off and was about to climb out of the car when Mandy grabbed his arm.

"Maybe we shouldn't go," Mandy said. "I don't want you to be uncomfortable."

"Mandy, baby." He cupped her cheek. "I'm not uncomfortable with this. I promise. They're our family."

"But you're not wearing your leather cut." She had a little pout to her lips.

"It is one of the things I miss. I'd have loved to see you naked and strutting around our place in it." He kissed her. "I love you, and I love my club."

"I want you to be happy. That's all I want."

"And I am." He pressed his head to hers. "Come on, let's go and mingle."

Climbing out of the car, he moved to her side and helped her out. She took his hand, and together they walked around toward where the barbeque was going on. Devil had his youngest daughter Ameila on his hip.

Kids were wandering around. Not only were there

club brothers but friends of the club as well. He spotted a couple of the strippers from Naked Fantasies, and the feeling of family was thick in the air. He tightened his grip around her wrist, not wanting to let go.

"You made it," Mia said, coming toward them.

Mandy was suddenly pulled into a hug, and then he was.

"Of course they would come. There's no way that anyone would turn down a club barbeque, especially with my man controlling the grill," Lexie said.

"I'll go and get you a drink," Mandy said, kissing his cheek before she disappeared. He watched her go and turned toward Lexie.

"How have you been?"

"I've been really good. What about you?"

"Good."

"You don't look good without the leather though," Lexie said, touching his arm.

"Something had to give, and I'm sure Devil filled you in."

"He did. So, this thing with Mandy, is that the real deal?" Lexie asked.

He was about to speak when Devil moved up toward his wife. "Good to have you here."

They shook hands, and Ameila reached out toward him.

"You want to go to Butler, sweetheart?" Devil asked.

Before he knew what was happening, Ameila was in his arms, and he smiled into the little girl's face, who let out a little giggle.

"She's growing up so fast," he said.

"They all do. Simon's already writing his wedding vows," Devil said.

Lexie chuckled.

"Speaking of vows, I'm marrying Mandy."

"Congratulations," Lexie said.

"Oh, she doesn't know we're marrying yet. I was hoping … if you don't mind … could you guys help me organize something really romantic?" he asked. Since their trip away, he'd been thinking about how he'd propose.

For this he wanted one special evening, twinkling lights, romantic dinner, soft music.

Lexie looked toward Devil. "I can help."

"Come, talk to me," Devil said.

He put Ameila in Lexie's arms and followed Devil toward the grill. There was already chicken cooking away, and he had three grills set up.

"How have you been?" Devil asked.

"I've been doing a lot of thinking, and Dick told me about what happened. The deal he has with you."

"He did? That does surprise me."

"I want you to do the same to me."

Devil turned toward him now, staring at him. "You do realize that Dick has never once gone back on the drugs."

"I didn't want the fucking drugs, I realize that now. I wasn't going to take them."

"The temptation wasn't there?"

"It's always fucking there. It would be a hell of a lot easier to just take them and have you put a bullet in my head, but that's before I had Mandy. She's … everything. The club has been my family, and I didn't think that I was needed here. We're settled, everything is taken care of, and you didn't need me. It's stupid and fucking childish, but that was the way it was. I didn't think you needed me, and I couldn't have Mandy. She was always there and out of reach."

"You had to fight for her, Butler. The moment

you did, everything fell into place."

Devil reached out, and he saw him pull a leather jacket from out of the cooler. "This is your cut."

"You're giving it back?"

"You didn't take the drugs, Butler. You had a minor setback while you got your shit together. You ever take, I'll be burying you in this. The club, your woman, our very future needs you. Your place is right here, and it has been for over twenty years, Butler. We go way fucking back, you and me. We rode together, partied together, got shitfaced together. You lost your way, and I get it, I do." He turned to look toward Lexie, who was surrounded by their children. "That woman … she loves me. Me! She wants me in her life. After everything I've done, and there is no second guessing that. She is my entire world, as is this club. They come together like peas in a fucking pod. There is a place here, man. If you want it."

He stared down at the jacket. It was like a lifeline.

"Mandy is mine."

"Of course. You can't keep your eyes off her. It took you long enough to claim her."

"You told me to keep my hands off the cleaner."

"Sometimes you have to fight for the shit you want in life. You're going to marry her, and that's all right with me."

Holding open the jacket, Butler stared at his patch, and as he slipped it back on, everything felt right in his world, finally. The leather fit against his skin, and even in the heat, he didn't feel too hot or scratchy. This was his cut, his place in the club.

Mandy came out, holding two sodas for the both of them.

He held his arms open, and she stepped between them.

"Hey, handsome. I almost didn't recognize you there with all that leather."

He tilted her head back, claiming her lips. There was a chorus of cheers as the club erupted, and he laughed.

"Is it like this all the time?"

"No. It's not." Pulling his leather cut from his body, he placed it over her shoulders. "I knew you'd look sexy as hell."

She rolled her eyes. "You could stand the heat, but it's a little hot for me."

He took the soda from her, and it wasn't long before Sasha was pulling her away. He sipped at his drink and watched as the old ladies enfolded her into the group.

"She blends in well," Devil said.

"She's a good woman. The best."

"I'll agree to disagree on that point."

"All of our women are the best," Butler said, laughing.

"So, remember that invitation that got canceled?"

"Which one? The Billionaire Bikers one? The posers?"

"The very ones."

Butler rubbed the back of his head. He didn't like the idea of going to an MC gathering, especially when it was hosted by a bunch of men who made more money than all of them combined.

"You're thinking of going?"

"With our new endeavor of being good little bikers, I thought it would be worth a shot seeing what they had to offer."

"And?"

"And I want you to come along. Family is invited, but I don't know if I want to risk it."

Butler started laughing. "No man in his right mind would take his family to a big, full-on event like this. All it will be is a bunch of men from all the clubs around, and I don't know."

"It will suck big time, I know."

"I'll come. It'll be interesting to see what billionaires think they can handle the MC." He finished off his soda and glanced at Mandy. "She really does look great."

"She's family, Butler. Just like you are."

"I see you got your shit together," Dick said, joining in the conversation.

Dick slapped him on the back, and it took all his restraint not to punch him. He had to remember Dick's words of wisdom even if he didn't like it.

"Yeah, I got my shit together."

"Good. The club isn't the same without you, man." Another slap to the back, and Dick moved away.

"If you're wanting to kill him right now, then you know you're back in the fold." Devil flipped the chicken, and he sipped at his drink. Lexie gave him the thumbs-up, and Mandy was laughing.

Life was really good.

****

Mandy checked the time once again and cursed that she had listened to Butler's promise to be back in time. Lexie had needed to leave for some family thing, and she'd offered to stay late at the shop.

"Come on, Butler, where are you?"

After twenty minutes of waiting for her ride, she was at the end of her patience. Crossing the street, she began the long journey home. At least she'd been wearing pumps for this and not heels. She never wore heels on the job. She believed they were the worst curse of all.

Sending him another text, she hoped it would beep with a message that he was late but coming. Nothing.

She got nothing, and it annoyed her.

He was finally back with Chaos Bleeds, and already he was ditching her.

Keep calm.

Keep cool.

After walking for forty minutes, she got to her building. She had already planned how she was going to yell at Butler and make him sorry for believing he could be reliable. She stomped all the way upstairs, and as she made it outside of her apartment, she stopped. A foot from the door were rose petals. Bending down, she picked up one of the petals and stroked the softness between her fingers.

There were so many of them, all over the place.

As she opened the door, soft music filled the air, and she stared at the path of rose petals.

"Hello," she said, stepping into her apartment.

Closing the door behind her, she was careful, not wanting to mess up the beautiful display spread out for her.

Rounding the corner, she came to a stop. There were no blaring lights, but so many candles, all of them lit and twinkling.

Butler stood near the table. He wore a tuxedo, and the scents of the food made her stomach growl. He held a bottle of sparkling water, and some passion fruit concentrate. She didn't have any alcohol in their apartment. He told her he didn't mind if she wanted to get some, but she had merely shaken her head.

Alcohol didn't mean anything to her. She liked water and soda a lot more. Butler on the other hand, he meant the world to her, and she found giving up alcohol an easy sacrifice to make.

"What is all this?"

"I wanted to share a romantic gesture with you."

"Okay. I'm quite easy. Picking me up would have been very romantic," she said.

"I know, but we had to finish here."

"We?"

"I got Lexie and a couple of the other old ladies to help me. I wanted this to be perfect."

He poured them both out a drink, and she watched as he held a chair out. "Come and sit."

Putting her bag on the floor, she stepped toward him, taking a seat at the table. He slid the chair underneath the table, and she took a sip of the drink. It was fruity and delicious. "You certainly know how to surprise a girl."

"I wanted to be there, and, standing here knowing that you were walking home, well, it was hard. I had Pussy follow you though. Sasha got him to do it so I knew you were safe."

"I had no idea someone was following me."

"Pussy's always been able to do that. It's his trick."

"I don't know if I like that but okay."

"I'll be right back," Butler said.

She watched him leave and stared at the table, the drinks, the lights, the flowers. It was all out of some kind of movie scene, and her heart pounded because of it.

Butler returned seconds later with her food, juicy steaks with potatoes and beans. The seasoned herb butter melted on top, and her mouth watered.

"Lexie helped with this as well."

"I love Lexie."

She cut into the steak, took a bite, and closed her eyes. The flavor was intense, juicy, and so perfect. She couldn't imagine eating anything else, ever again. "This is just perfect."

"I know, right? Lexie taught me, and whenever I'm in the doghouse, expect this kind of food. I'm totally going to rock your world."

"You are?"

"Yes, I am."

They kept on eating, and all the time, her curiosity was getting the better of her. She didn't want to spoil it though.

Butler had told her himself that he wasn't about the romance, and yet this was proof he was.

"I thought you didn't like romance?" she asked, finally spilling out the words. She couldn't handle the secrets and hated not knowing what was going on.

"I like romance, but I don't think it should come with any other symbol. Not chocolate or jewelry, even though that has its place."

She took another bite of her steak, washing it down with some of her fruit juice, and stared at him. "I … what is going on?"

He'd said that he loved her, and her feelings had only deepened as they spent more time together.

Butler took her hand, and he was suddenly down on one knee beside her at the table. "I don't want to break up with you, Mandy. Far from it, okay. I wanted all of this because I know you've never had anyone care enough to give you romance. I love you more than anything, and I want to provide for you, to give you everything your heart desires, and to never stop doing that."

"Okay."

"Shit, I'm doing all this wrong." She watched him reach into his pocket, and as he did, he returned his gaze to her. "There's no one else that I want to spend the rest of my life with. I love you, Mandy, flaws and all. Just like I know you love me. I don't have a squeaky-clean past, or at times even a budding future. I make messes of everything, and I ... am probably the least romantic person in Chaos Bleeds for you to fall for. Even Dick knows what he's doing, but not me."

She chuckled. She couldn't help it. He looked so sweet, so charming, and utterly lost.

"But ... I will do whatever it takes to win you, to have you in my life. I can take whatever everyone else throws at me, but losing you, I can't handle that. When you were gone, I tried to get over that. I didn't know where you were, but I thought about you every single second of every single day, and those kinds of feelings never disappear, not once. I love you more than anything. I thought love, a family, a life outside of the MC wouldn't happen for me, but when I'm with you, I want it all. I want you to be my wife, Mandy, the mother of my kids, and for us to get married, and I'm really fucking frustrated right now because I have the damn box in my pocket and I can't get it out, and I want to do the romantic thing but I can't."

Mandy laughed, and in order for them to get the velvet box out of his jeans, they had to cut away the pocket.

"See, I blew it, completely blew it."

She cupped his face, kissing him deeply. "Get down on one knee and finish it."

Butler slid to the floor, box in hand, and he opened it up. The engagement ring was stunning, beautiful, and everything she didn't even realize that she wanted.

"Mandy, will you do me the honor of becoming my wife?"

"Yes."

"Yes?"

She nodded her head, holding her hand out as he slid the ring on her finger, which was a perfect fit.

He pulled her into his arms and she closed her eyes, loving his touch around her. She loved him so much.

"I wanted this to be perfect."

"Stop worrying, Butler. This *is* perfect, and I know I will never, ever forget this proposal, not ever." She cupped his face, kissing him again. "I never thought I could love anyone as much as I love you."

"Good, because I intend to make you feel that for the rest of our lives."

"You promise?"

"It's a guarantee."

****

Billionaire Bikers Picnic

"What do you think?" Lash asked.

"I don't know, and I don't trust it." Devil wrinkled his nose, not really sure what to do.

"The invite said we should bring our families."

"Do you really want to take that risk?" Tiny asked.

"They've got a unicorn stand. Who the fuck gives unicorns at an MC meeting?" Butler asked.

Devil glanced around the large field. The house they'd been invited to was huge and looked more like a mansion than a home. Stands were set up, and the actual picnic looked out of place, especially as he spotted several MCs each in their groups. He saw the Trojans MC, Dirty Fuckers, Saints and Sinners, then of course there was them, The Skulls and Chaos Bleeds MC.

Their reputation for sticking together was why both clubs had ridden together today. Lash had been by his side with several of their club at their backs.

He could just see his little girls squealing with delight over the teddy bear stand.

"I feel like I've walked into an alternate reality right now," Dick said. "Everything looks … weird."

"Then blink."

His hand was on his gun, poised and ready as the Billionaire Bikers made their way out. They were dressed in suits, all ten of them. He spotted three of the men with their old ladies, but that still wasn't enough for him to back down.

"Welcome," Russ said.

Devil made it his business to know every single MC Prez. He could spot them in every single MC here.

"You do realize the fucking risks here, right?" Duke asked. "Or do you think you're above such risks with your money?"

"I don't think that at all. None of us do. I know that to many of you our club is a mockery, but I promise you it isn't. There's something I want."

"Dirty Fuckers don't play this game, we never have," James said.

Saint remained silent. Devil waited, and when Russ turned to look at him, he knew business was about to go down.

"I know it was a long shot with the other clubs, but I want to let you all know that we know about your current alliance. We want to talk business, plans, and a future that can help many people, not just our clubs."

Devil glanced at Lash then back at Russ. He knew what the club was talking about. "We're listening."

"Good, this is not a joke. We'd very much like for you to invite your families. This is a sign that we are no threat to you."

Grabbing his cell phone, Devil dialed Lexie's number. "Babe, how would you like to make a day of it?"

Epilogue

Three years later

Mandy moaned as Butler kissed a path down her neck, and she giggled. It had been too long since he'd kissed her, made love to her. Of course, they had the best reason for not having two minutes together.

In fact, as his hand settled between her thighs, the soft sounds of their little girl filled the air. Butler groaned, his face dropping against her ass.

"I think it's feeding time," Mandy said.

"Do you have to?"

"Yes, I do. You know I do."

He rolled off her back, and she leaned over, kissing his lips. She caught a glimpse of his wedding band, and still, even after three years, she found it to be the best sight. Her ownership of him.

"Come back soon," he said.

"I will." Another kiss, and she left the bed.

Entering the small nursery that all of the Chaos Bleeds crew had made up, she moved toward the crib. "Hello, my beautiful, baby Christie," she said. "You are being a big giant pain, but I don't mind. No, I don't." She spoke in a baby voice as she picked up her little girl.

Christie was only three months old, and one of the most precious people in her world. After they had gotten married the same year he proposed, neither of them was in a rush for a family. Instead they enjoyed married life, and she adjusted to her place as part of the club. Being an old lady wasn't easy, not at all.

To the outside world, a lot of people probably assumed that besides handling food and dealing with their men that was where life ended, but it wasn't. They were there for everything and for each other. Whether it be for birthday parties, babysitting, dealing with the business ventures, all of it was part and parcel of being an old lady. Not only were they there for each other, but also The Skulls, and they had been through a lot in the past couple of years.

Mandy held her baby girl closer to her. "I'm never going to let anything happen to you. You know that, don't you? Nothing."

Christie nuzzled her breast and she helped, watching her little girl suckle.

"That is a beautiful sight," Butler said.

She knew he wouldn't stay away long. Even when she'd been giving birth, he'd started off the labor process outside of her room. By the end, he was on the bed, and she'd rested against him, and together they worked to bring their little girl into the world.

He moved toward her, sitting on the little stool. "I still can't believe that's our little girl."

"We made something beautiful together," Mandy said.

With her free hand, she took hold of his, and like so many times before, they locked fingers.

He kissed her knuckles. "You coming in my room that day changed my entire world."

Tears flooded her eyes. Love filled every single part of her. This was her little family, but they were part of a much bigger one.

"I don't want you to cry," Butler said.

"They are happy tears, so happy. You give me everything, Butler. A loving husband, a beautiful little girl, a family, a place to call my own. I love you more than anything in the world."

He got to his feet and cupped her cheek. "And I will keep on giving to you for the rest of our life."

"Till death do we part?" she asked.

"Even then, if I'm gone, I'll still be waiting for

you."

The End

www.samcrescent.com

EVERNIGHT PUBLISHING ®

www.evernightpublishing.com

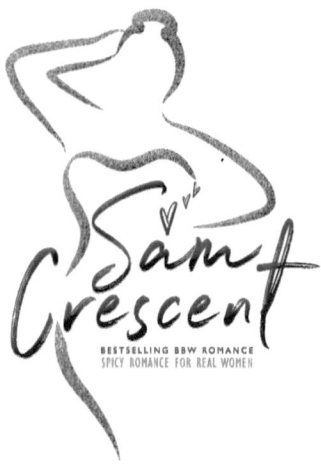